VEGAS
MOON

John Locke is a *New York Times* bestselling author, and was the first self-published author in history to hit the number 1 spot on Kindle. He is the author of the Donovan Creed and Emmett Love series. He lives in Kentucky.

D0280425

worthy of 6 Stars! By TRW

I give 5 stars to all John Locke books, I would give 6 stars to this one if I could. Not only is it a page turning thriller – I read the whole thing on the beach in an afternoon – couldn't put it down.

***** A fun read! By Kathy

This novel is chock-full of surprising plot twists and turns from beginning to end. It grips you from page one. I read this book in one evening. It's a fast, fun read for sure.

***** Bingo! Cool. Read this book and you're hooked on Locke. By Karin

Locke keeps the story moving and in such an effortless way. I'm passing it on to my husband. It's been awhile since I've read something sexy; this fits the bill.

***** So Entertaining I just went and downloaded another one.
By Patti Roberts

I read this book over a period of 2 days on my Kindle and loved it! So I have just downloaded another one. I hereby declare that I am a John Locke fan. Do yourself a favor....

***** Life equals Experimentation.
By Jean I just couldn't put the book down. Must Read!

***** 10 stars. By Ally

A wonderful mystery thriller. I love all of them but I think this is just my favorite.

AMAZON.COM

THE DONOVAN CREED SERIES

VEGAS
MOON
JOHN LOCKE

HEAD
ZEUS

This edition first published in the UK in 2013 by Head of Zeus Ltd

9 7 5 3 1 2 4 6 8

A CIP catalogue record for this book is available from
the British Library.

ISBN (Paperback): 9781781852422
ISBN (eBook): 9781781852439

Printed and bound by CPI Group (UK) Ltd, Croydon, CR0 4YY

Head of Zeus Ltd
Clerkenwell House
45-47 Clerkenwell Green
London EC1R 0HT

www.headofzeus.com

VEGAS
MOON

PROLOGUE

I

JIM "LUCKY" PETERS was in Jamaica, getting a colonoscopy from a Rastafarian proctologist, when his cell phone started buzzing.

"Wha's that, Hon?" the doctor said to his nurse. "Some sarta buzzin' sound."

She located Lucky's cell phone, frowned, confiscated it. Lucky was half-conscious, and loopy enough from the "relaxing" medicine not to care. What he did care about was whatever the hell Dr. Gayle was doing in his lower tract.

"You're gonta feel some pressure, now, Mon," he said.

Pressure?

Understatement.

Was Dr. Gayle drilling for oil? Impaling him through the ass with a flagpole?

"If you're looking for Jimmy Hoffa, I can tell you right now, he's not in there," Lucky said, through clenched teeth.

"Who's Jimmy Hoffa, Mon?"

"Seriously. You push that thing any deeper, you'll scratch the back of my eyeballs!"

"Almost done, Mon, and clean as a whistle she is."

The pain and suffering was all on Lucky, since he decided to forego the anesthetic. Like all his decisions, this one had

1

been a calculated risk.

Lucky Peters knows a lot about risk. And reward, and odds of every sort. He's a legendary gambler, allegedly worth something above fifty million dollars, the man Las Vegas casinos fear more than any other. More than they used to fear the mob, even. When Lucky sets the line on a game, casino owners hold their breath. When he wins, they shit their pants. On any given day of the week, Lucky's got a million bucks riding the line. And three times that on the weekend. And historically, sixty-eight percent of the time he wins.

Lucky's success is based on vigilance, and keeping up with the constant flux in the betting landscape. Case in point: last time he went under the knife he accepted the anesthetic, missed the injury report on Packer cornerback Johnny Sullivan, and it cost him eighty large!

So, never again.

One p.m., still in Kingston Hospital but significantly recovered, Lucky located his cell phone among his belongings and saw he had four messages, all from world-renowned plastic surgeon, Dr. Phyllis Willis. Lucky pressed the replay button to retrieve the first one.

"Lucky, this is Phyllis. Connor Payne is in the lobby of my practice! What should I do? Please call me back!" Dr. Willis sounded frantic.

Suddenly Lucky wasn't feeling so lucky. A cold chill swept through his body. Connor Payne was an international assassin. If he was in Dr. Willis's lobby, it could only mean he had information that could eventually lead to Lucky.

Second message started.

"My receptionist told Connor Payne I'm in the middle of a procedure. He doesn't believe her. He's giving me two minutes to come out, then he's coming to get me. Should I call

2

the police? I don't know what to do! I'm terrified. Please call!"

Lucky closed his eyes. This didn't sound good.

Third message came on.

"I'm making a corporate decision. I'm in the bathroom, the door's locked. I've got the controller. I'm going to punch in the code and melt his brain right where he stands. I can't see any other way out of this. Okay, I'm hanging up. I'm going to do it. Please forgive me!"

Lucky pressed the pause button, thinking, Please don't kill him. They'll do an autopsy and find the chip we implanted in his brain. On the other hand, Dr. Phyllis Willis was a surgeon. Maybe she could slice his head open and retrieve the chip before anyone finds out what killed him.

Lucky shook his head. That was ridiculous. First of all, the receptionist, Shelby, was a witness. Second, there'd be no reason for Phyllis to slice open the brain of a man who suddenly died in the lobby of her building. If pressed by the police, Phyllis would crack and tell everything she knew. Lucky had half his life's savings invested in Ropic Industries, a company whose stock had been slipping for months. This type of news could send it into free fall.

Lucky noted the time of the calls. All four were back-to-back, made in the space of three minutes. He reminded himself that whatever he was about to hear had taken place two hours ago. It had already happened, and there was nothing he could do now, but listen how it played out. Lucky took a deep breath, hit the play button on his cell phone.

"Mr. Peters, I-I entered the code. I entered the code, b-but he's still alive! He's moving through the office! I-I think he may have killed Shelby! Oh, dear God! There are five people here. Connor Payne is going to kill us all! I can't believe you never called me back! I'm going to die today."

Phyllis paused a moment, then said, "I need to tell you something. Two things. First, I don't regret our affair. I'm glad we did it, because…well, because I love you. I always have and always will. And second, you need to know where I hid the device. Since the code didn't work, you'll need the device to re-set it."

Phyllis paused again, as if listening for Connor Payne. Then she whispered, "Don't be angry. What I did was really stupid, but—"

On the phone, Phyllis suddenly went into full-blown panic mode. "Shit! Here he comes! I—I love you, Lucky!"

II

LUCKY NEEDED TO…not panic. He tried not panicking for awhile, but his heart was racing a mile a minute. He decided to think, instead. Okay, so he needed to make some calls.

Several calls. How many, exactly?

Three.

But who first?

Phyllis? His wife, Gwen? Mob boss Carmine Porrello?

Phyllis's cell phone went unanswered. When he called her office, a cop said, "This is Detective Scrapple. I'm logging calls for Dr. Willis. Could you state your name, please, and your relationship to Dr. Willis?"

Lucky hung up. He knew it was a stupid thing to do, since Phyllis's cell phone records would show he was the last person she called before her murder. Assuming she's dead.

Assuming?

Of course she's dead! Or she'd have called him.

Damn good thing I can prove I was in Jamaica when it happened, he thought. Of course, the details of his affair with Phyllis might come to light. Then again, beyond the cold shoulder he could expect from Gwen, a public affair could enhance his reputation as a lady's man. A plus, in a town like Vegas.

If Lucky was anything, he was lucky. He calculated the odds of surviving Phyllis's murder relatively unscathed, and put them at 12 to 1.

Connor Payne was a different matter.

Did Phyllis tell him about Lucky's connection to the device? If so, Lucky and Gwen were both in danger.

Lucky called Gwen's cell.

No answer.

He tried their home.

No answer.

This was a problem. If Gwen's cell phone was operating, her voice message would have come on. He caught himself wishing he'd taken Gwen to Jamaica. It would've been nice to have a friendly face here, but he'd wanted to sample the local talent. He didn't get far with the Jamaican women, though. In fact, he never got started. Because by the time he landed he was already shitting blood through his shorts. After gagging everyone in first class and then baggage claim, Lucky caught a cab and went straight to the hospital. After a day of tests and prep, they scheduled his colonoscopy. Welcome to the Islands, indeed, Lucky thought.

His third call got a response.

Mob boss Carmine "The Chin" Porrello couldn't wait to take Lucky's call. He'd been trying to infiltrate Lucky's sports betting empire for years. But so far, Lucky had managed to resist the charms of doing business with the mob.

"What's up?" Carmine said.

"You know this hit man, Connor Payne?"

"Never heard of him."

"Really?"

"Really. Why you askin'?"

"He might be after me."

"Sounds like you got a problem."

"I need a bodyguard."

"If your boy's for real, none a' my people are gonna want the job."

"I just need a name. Who's the best hit man in the business?"

"By business, you mean the family?"

"No. In the world. Is there someone who's considered the best in the world?"

"Only one can be the best. But you'll never get him."

"Why?"

"He don't need the money."

Lucky said, "You give me the name, I'll get him to work for me."

"Things like this ain't free."

"You can't give me a flippin' name?"

"Not this name. Not for free."

"Fine. How much?"

"Ten."

"Ten grand? For a name?"

"Yeah, that's right. But it's a helluva name. Someone asks you for it, you can get your money back."

"Yeah, but ten g's?"

"Ten. Nothing less."

"Fuck. Okay, done. What's the name?"

Carmine's voice went low. "My part ends when I say the name. You don't tell no one I gave it to you, *capisca*?"

"Fine. What's the name?"

Carmine paused, as if looking around before saying it. "Donovan Creed," he whispered.

"What's his number?"

"What? You think I know his fuckin' number?"

"What'd I just pay you ten large for, if not his number?"

"His name, asshole."

"How am I going to find his number?" Lucky said.

"That'll cost you."

"How much?"

"Five more."

"You gotta be shitting me."

"Let me tell you somethin', Lucky."

"Yeah?"

"When someone wants this man's name and number, they're humpin' their last chicken."

Lucky paused. "I don't have any idea what you just said."

"Ah, shit. I'm gettin' old. There's an expression in there somewhere. I just can't remember the fuckin' thing. You want the number, or what?"

"Yeah, fine."

Carmine gave a number.

"What's this, his cell phone?"

"No. Sal Bonadello's."

"Who the fuck is that?" Lucky said.

"The guy that can get you Creed."

III

IT COSTS LUCKY another ten grand to finally get Donovan Creed on the phone. When he does, it goes like this:

"Mr. Creed, this is Jim Peters, from Las Vegas. My friends call me Lucky."

Dead silence.

"Are you there?"

"Sorry, I thought you were making a speech."

"Where are you, Mr. Creed? I mean, are you in the States?"

"Mr. Peters, I'll be glad to tell you where I am, but it'll cost you an ear."

"A...what? Did you say an ear? What are you talking about?"

"You want something personal from me, I get something of yours in return. Since you asked, I'm in—"

"Shit no!" Lucky screams. "Don't tell me!"

The voice on the other end is calm. "Fair enough. Why are we speaking today?"

"Ever hear of a guy named Connor Payne?"

"I have."

"What do you know about him?"

"He's one of the most lethal people in the world. Why do you ask?"

"I have reason to believe he murdered a friend of mine a few hours ago."

"A close friend?"

"Well...yes. I mean, she was the Medical Director of a corporation I invested in. I'm the majority stockholder."

"Wow. So Connor Payne murdered your friend."

"Yes."

"What are you going to do about it?"

"Me? I...well...I mean, I'm trying to do something about it right now. By calling you."

"Did you have sex with her just the two times, or has this been going on awhile?"

"I—what? No. I mean, we did business together. We had a professional relationship."

"Are you telling me Phyllis Willis was a hooker?"

"What? No, of course not. I mean, wait—how did you know her name?"

"It's my job to know. By the way, were you able to keep your polyp?"

"My...polyp? What polyp?"

"The one Dr. Gayle cut out of your colon this morning."

"He...I mean...what?"

Creed made a tsk, tsk sound. "Let me guess: he told you there was nothing in there."

"His exact words were, I was clean as a whistle."

"He keeps them, you know."

"Polyps?"

"Yup."

"Why?"

"Makes necklaces out of them. Sells them on the Broomilaw."

"The Broomilaw?"

"When it ices over. Between bear fights."

This conversation has completely gotten away from Lucky. He starts over. "Mr. Creed, I want to hire you."

"You want me to get your polyp back?"

"I want you to protect me from Connor Payne."

"Whew."

"Excuse me?"

"Thank God you're asking for something simple."

"Simple?"

"Compared to getting your polyp back."

Lucky was getting frustrated. "Are you sure you're Donovan Creed?"

"Pretty sure."

"The Donovan Creed who kills people?"

"Are you recording this conversation?"

"Of course not!"

"Too bad. I've been working on my tough-guy voice. I was hoping to hear how it comes across over the phone."

"Mr. Creed."

"Yes?"

"I'm a wealthy man. I can pay you to protect me. How much would you charge?"

"Depends on what you want. Do I just have to keep you alive, or would I have to kill Connor Payne?"

"You...could kill him?"

"I could. But I doubt I'll have to."

"Why not?"

"If he knows I'm guarding you, he won't come within ten miles of us."

"If that's true, I shouldn't have to pay you very much," Lucky said.

"That's a rather odd way to look at it."

11

"I'll pay you twenty grand a week. How does that sound?"

"Paltry."

"Are you kidding me?"

"A premium hooker would cost you thirty. And offer no protection against Connor Payne."

"I don't need a hooker."

"You might, if you're right about Phyllis being dead."

Lucky sighed. "Look. You want the job or not?"

"Mr. Peters?"

"Yeah?"

"You're a liar, a cheat, and a cheapskate."

"Based on?"

"You lied about fucking Phyllis. You cheated on your wife. And you don't want to pay me a fair price to save your life."

Lucky paused. When he spoke, he sounded dejected. "How'd you know about Phyllis?"

"Carmine told me."

"Carmine Porrello?"

"You know any other Carmines?"

"He said he didn't know you! That sonofabitch charged me fifteen grand for Sal's phone number! And Sal charged me ten for yours!"

"So you'll pay twenty-five grand to get me on the phone, but only twenty a week to protect you? That hurts, Mr. Peters. If I have to seek therapy over this, who's going to stop Connor Payne from killing you?"

"I can kill him myself."

"Now that's a bold statement."

"There's a device. I only need you as long as it takes to find it."

"Interesting. Tell me more."

"I can't. Not over the phone. If you protect Gwen till I get back to Vegas, you and I can search Phyllis's office together, and find this thing I'm looking for."

"Gwen?"

"My wife. Her life could be in danger."

"Why?"

"If Connor Payne thinks I have the device, he might go to my house looking for it."

"Or for you."

"Right."

"But you don't have it."

"No. Phyllis has…had it."

"Want me to check her office?"

"You can't. The police are there. You can get me in there tonight, though, right?"

"If I come to Vegas," Creed said.

Lucky said, "How did Carmine know about Phyllis?"

"Mr. Peters, you may be brilliant when it comes to bookmaking, but you don't know shit about the people who are scheming to bring you down."

"And you do?"

"What I don't know I can figure out."

"But you won't help me."

"Did I say that?"

"You said I was a liar, a cheat, and a cheapskate."

"True. Nevertheless, I'm in."

"You are?"

"I'm intrigued."

"Why?"

"Connor Payne is a one-man army. I want to know how you plan to kill him."

"I'll tell you tonight, after I land. There's a direct flight to Vegas, leaves at five, gets there nine twenty. I need you to go to my house, watch my wife till then."

"Okay."

"And bring her with you to the airport to meet my plane."

"You need to let her know I'm coming."

"Of course."

"There's one problem."

"What?"

"The police are having a convention at your house."

"How do you know?"

"Carmine told me."

Lucky's heart sinks. "You don't think something's happened to Gwen, do you?"

"No."

"You sure?"

"Positive."

"Why?"

"No ambulance."

"Mr. Creed. Are you in fact in Las Vegas?"

"Let's put it like this: I can be at your house in an hour."

"And you'll take the job?"

"If you agree to cooperate."

"What would I have to do?"

"Tell me everything."

"Everything?"

"That's right."

"About Connor Payne?"

"We can start with him and see where it takes us."

"Fine. But I can't divulge any details about my business."

"Why not?"

"It could ruin me."

"Let me put it this way. You can tell me what I want to know, or you can tell Connor Payne everything. And he won't ask nicely."

1.

29 Hours Earlier...

THE CHIP IN my head can be activated by tapping a four-digit code into a device that looks like a wristwatch. When the code is entered, the chip heats up and starts liquefying my brain. Do that to me, and you better have fresh batteries and type in the right code, because if you don't, I'm going to come for you.

It's not personal.

I know you've got a life, a loving spouse, two apple-cheeked kids, three dogs, four cats and five parakeets. Or maybe you live alone in a basement apartment with a single window that's half dirt and half sky, and you dine nightly on canned cat food while fantasizing about large, hairy women in boxer shorts who could win the limbo contest if the people on either end would just raise the fucking bar!

Either way, you've got a life, and as far as I'm concerned, you deserve to live it without interference from me.

Until you press those buttons.

Do that, and your life belongs to me.

I'm Donovan Creed, former CIA assassin, sometime hit man for the mob. I currently head up a team of assassins who kill suspected terrorists for Uncle Sam. I can be your best friend or your worst nightmare.

But you should know I don't have many friends.

I'm a tolerant, even-tempered guy who likes the same things you do: long walks on the beach at sunset, holding hands, romantic candle-lit dinners featuring great food and premium Kentucky bourbon, making love under the stars with high-end call girls, torturing, maiming and killing bad guys...

I'm not a bully.

Random comment, I know, but God, I hate bullies.

I've been told I have a hero complex, which means I feel compelled to help those in need. Personally, I think the world would be a better place if more people get involved when bad things go down. But apparently the fact I feel compelled to help people—instead of choosing to help them—makes me something of a sociopath. Let's say it this way: if you're a bully—and that word covers a lot of ground with me—it won't take long for you to see something no one wants to see:

The man I keep hid.

To prevent that from happening, don't fuck with the USA, and don't fuck with me, or the people I care about.

Which brings me to the buzz I felt in my head a few hours ago. The one caused not by alcohol, but by someone attempting to activate the kill chip in my brain.

I'd been enjoying a lovely dinner with Miranda, a particularly attractive young lady of the evening. We were in New York City, had the whole night ahead of us. I didn't cancel the date, because we'd been looking forward to it for weeks. In the end, we had a great time despite the fact someone was trying to kill me.

Here's what I know about the kill chip: it was grafted to my brain more than a year ago by the government surgeon who heads the hospital at Sensory Resources, a secret facility in north-west Virginia, where I have an office and a jail cell I sleep in from time to time. By choice. Doc Howard implanted the chip while I was in a coma, under his care. Unfortunately, it can't be removed without rendering me brain dead. When I found out what he'd done, guess what I did about it?

Nothing.

Crazy, right? But as it turned out, Doc had been following orders from my boss, Darwin, who wanted the means to snuff me at will. By telling me about the chip, Doc Howard did me a favor, though he charged me a hundred million dollars. He gave me a controller, the code, and showed me how to change it. As a plus, he explained that if Darwin ever tried to kill me, I'd feel a buzzing in my head.

But the buzzing I felt at dinner had nothing to do with Darwin. I know, because the device requires GPS, and Darwin was in an underground bunker all night, hosting a Homeland Security meeting.

Miranda gives me a long, sensual kiss and asks me to stay. I know it's part of the service, and she doesn't mean it, but it's nice to hear, anyway. I mean, she obviously likes me more than she has to, but I maintain no illusions about our relationship. It's tit for cash. Still, had the attempt on my life not been made, I would've stayed.

I love falling asleep in a woman's arms.

Reluctantly, I leave Miranda's house and walk to my limo. After getting comfortable, I call Doc Howard, who predictably complains about the time of night. I tell him about the buzzing in my head earlier, and he says he'll look into it.

I say, "Look into it now, because I'm coming to see you."

I get Lou Kelly, my facilitator, to book me a jet helicopter. He does, but it won't be ready for two hours. My limo driver takes me back to the hotel to pack my bags and check out.

Then we wait an hour by the private airstrip till the chopper shows up.

An hour after that I land on the Sensory Resources helipad. I have enough time to take a shower and drink a protein shake before meeting with Doc Howard. When he finally arrives, I start right in on him. "Two weeks ago I wired a hundred million to your offshore account in return for a bypass code."

"Yes." Doc Howard is visibly nervous, as he should be. Who can blame him? I'm not happy.

"You told me no one else had access to the code," I say, knowing that's not entirely true.

"I said to the best of my knowledge no one had it, but if someone did, and tried to access it, you'd feel buzzing in your head."

"Only problem is, I don't know who pressed the button last night."

"I've been thinking about that," Doc said.

"And?"

"There was someone present when I implanted the chip."

"What? Who?"

"The medical director of the company that manufactured it."

"And you decided not to tell me this because?"

"I was afraid you'd kill her, to tie up the loose end."

"I didn't kill you."

"No, but at the time, I didn't know you could be reasoned with."

"I try to give people a chance, Doc."

"You would have killed her."

"Probably. In the end. I mean, I'm walking around with a bomb in my head and she's got the code that can set it off. She's a major threat."

"I didn't consider her a threat at the time."

"Because?"

"I thought she had no way to access the code, once we changed it."

"But that wasn't true, was it?"

"Apparently not. I think the company lied about the device."

"You're quite astute. I hadn't realized till now."

"I note your sarcasm," Doc Howard says. "But yes. There has to be a master device that can reset the code."

I shake my head.

"I'm sorry," he says.

"That's comforting."

Doc Howard is short, pudgy, middle-aged, with thick glasses and a kindly grandfather's face. He's looking at me with less fear than he'd shown earlier. He knows he's valuable to me for reasons that would take too long to list.

But I'll give you one: he does all our body-double surgeries. I've got people all over the country guarding other people who don't even know they're being guarded. They're body doubles for my hit squad, my family, my closest friends. I need Doc Howard, and we've always gotten along. I don't resent him charging me for sharing his secret. Proves he trusts me more than he trusts Darwin.

On the other hand, who wouldn't?

"I want names and addresses," I say.

"Her name is Phyllis Willis."

I look at him. "Don't make me lose my patience."

"Swear to God, that's her name: Dr. Phyllis Willis."

"And she works where?"

"Ropic Industries, Las Vegas."

"What do they do?"

"I don't know. Darwin set it up. I only know about the chip."

"Is Dr. Willis in-house?"

"No. She's a plastic surgeon."

"In Vegas?"

"I think so. But wherever she is, I'm sure Lou Kelly's guys can find her."

"We didn't have this conversation, Doc."

"Of course not."

I pause. "You should've told me."

"I was trying to save a life. I'm sorry."

I turn to leave. Doc Howard says, "Phyllis thinks your name is Connor Payne."

"What?"

"That's the name—"

I hold up my hand. "I remember. That's good. I can use it to my advantage."

He nods, relieved.

2.

CONNOR PAYNE IS the name Darwin gave me when I came out of the coma. He went to a great deal of trouble to legally "kill" Creed and establish Connor Payne as a living, breathing person with a full history, including phony medical and dental records. When I decided to keep my original name, Darwin was furious at my lack of appreciation. Nevertheless, he kept the identity active on the chance I might need it someday.

It's late afternoon.

I'm in Vegas, in the multi-million dollar high-rise condo Callie Carpenter shares with her life partner, Eva LeSage. Callie's my top operative, and at the risk of sounding like a Hollywood script, she's not only the deadliest woman I've ever met, but the most beautiful, as well. A natural blonde, Callie boasts the entire package: flawless skin, piercing eyes, high cheekbones, dazzling smile, smokin' hot body...and the most amazing mouth I've ever seen. Her lips...are stunning. Not enhanced, not thin, not pouty—Christ, I feel like a slow learner in a high-school writing class trying to come up with words that do them justice. I mean, can I buy a friggin' adjective that hasn't been overused?

I'll start over.

You know how some women look like moms, and some like teachers? And some look frigid, while others look bedtime? Well, Callie's mouth looks like heaven. It's an astonishing mouth, with lips so enticing they force your attention away from what is already a perfect woman.

Callie would never have to sell her body.

Men would pay to watch her apply lipstick.

Another great thing about Callie? She's a good sport, always up for a kill.

When I tell her about the chip she says, "We really need to do something about Darwin."

"It'll eventually come to that," I say.

We sit in silence awhile, thinking about killing Darwin. Then she says, "What about Phyllis?"

"I'm going to pay her a visit tonight."

"At her place?"

I nod.

"You think she's got the device?"

"No. But she'll know who does. Meanwhile, it's great having you on standby."

Callie shrugs. "It's something to do till the next assignment."

"Speaking of which..."

She looks up. "Yeah?"

"Darwin met with Homeland last night, so the next assignment could come any minute."

"Good."

I raise an eyebrow.

She responds, "Too much domestic bliss wears me down over time."

I smile. "Trouble in Paradise?"

She shrugs. "You know how it is, living full-time with a woman. Not to mention she's a trapeze artist, with aches and pains and the attitude you get with circus folk."

I look at her a minute.

"Do you guys ever..."

"What?"

I move my hand in a swaying motion, like a trapeze. Then say, "You know…"

"What're you, sixteen?" she says.

"Sometimes."

We're quiet a minute. Then I say, "Seriously, Callie, what's happened?"

"What do you mean?"

"Last time I was here you were walking on air. I'd never seen you so happy."

She stares at the window a moment, then stands and walks over to it and adjusts the blinds. Turns back to face me and says, "You know what I do all day?"

"I can only fantasize."

"I do absolutely nothing. Nothing but wait for your calls. I mean, I get up early, Eva's sleeping. I go for a run, or work out, or lay out by the pool, or go shopping, or get my hair and nails done, but nine times out of ten, I'm doing all those things alone."

"Could be worse though, right?"

"I'm bored out of my fucking skull! We can't go anywhere because Eva's life is wrapped up in that God-forsaken show. She sleeps till noon, rehearses till six, performs till ten."

"Doesn't she ever get a day off?"

"Tuesdays. But she's always recuperating from one thing or another. And lately, she's supposedly been visiting her mother Tuesday nights."

"You don't believe her?"

She sighs. "You don't want to hear all this bullshit, do you?"

"I do. You never talk about your personal life."

"Shows you how desperate I've become."

"You think she's cheating?"

"I...no. But she's distant. And last week when she went out, she took a bag."

"She spent the night?"

"No. But she didn't bring the bag back."

"Maybe she gave it to her mother."

"Maybe."

I study her face. "What have you done?"

She shakes her head. "God, I can't believe it's come to this."

"Tell me."

"I put a tracking device on her car."

"And if you find out she's cheating?"

She sighs again. "I've given up my days and nights for this woman. I moved away from my home in Georgia. You know how much I loved living on the lake."

"I do."

"It's not like I'm old, or ugly..."

"You're the most beautiful woman on the planet Earth."

"See?"

"If she's cheating on you, she doesn't deserve you."

"That's what I'm saying."

"And if she's not cheating?"

"Then I'm going to have a hell of a boring life."

"Until the next time I call."

"Until then."

"It's what you live for."

"No. Waiting for Eva to get in the mood is what I live for."

"Tell me what that's like. When she's in the mood."

"Donovan?"

"Yeah?"

"I mean this in all honesty."

"Go ahead."

"If I were to start telling you about it, you'd cream your jeans before I got to the good part."

I blink two, three times. Then say, "I love it when you talk dirty."

"You should hear me with Eva."

"Any chance of that happening?"

"No. You want a drink?"

"Maybe later. After my cold shower."

She smiles.

"Eva must be a helluva woman," I say, "especially in bed."

"She's a trapeze artist."

"And that makes a big difference, right? I mean, all jokes aside?"

She smiles. "You can't begin to comprehend."

"You sure about that?"

"Positive."

"How can you say that?"

"The fact you had to ask proves you have no point of reference from which to imagine it."

3.

PHYLLIS WILLIS IS thirty-eight years old and lives in a six-year-old, 4,600-square-foot home on a small piece of Henderson real estate, a few miles south-east of Vegas. The house is one-and-a-half stories, with three bedrooms and four baths. The two-car garage faces the street, and has an iron gate that closes to make a concrete courtyard. There's not much yard to maintain, but her lawn service does a good job. Personally, I think $260.00 a week is too much to pay for what she's getting. Then again, it's less than a Botox treatment.

The troubled economy has hit Phyllis's neighborhood hard. One out of every three houses is vacant, including the one to her right, which gives me a clear path to entry. You get a good feel for these things over time, so I know before breaking in that her house is empty. I did a walk-through anyway, before going through her desk and filing cabinet, where I found all the details about her house I told you about. In case you care, it set her back a cool seven-fifty. I wonder why a woman with no kids or husband would want such a large house.

I glance at her desktop. There's an art to piecing together a person's life by going through their personal effects. The bills stacked neatly on the left of her desk pad, ballpoint on the right, tells me she's right-handed. There's a small hand sanitizer with an orange top, and a colorful foam coaster beside it that appears to have been painted by a child. To the untrained eye, this probably means nothing.

I call Callie. When she answers, I say, "I'm in her house, but Phyllis isn't here."

"So?"

"She's having an affair with a Las Vegas gambler named Jim "Lucky" Peters. Ever hear of him?"

"Of course. He's like the most famous gambler in the world."

"Really?"

"Really."

"Does he win a lot?"

"Are you kidding me? He wins a million dollars a week, if the press can be trusted. He's got an army of weirdos all over the country who phone in data to him twenty-four seven."

"What kind of weirdos?"

"He claims he gets information from autistic savants, ball boys, drug dealers, steroid pushers, memorabilia salespeople, fitness trainers, hookers—you name it. And everyone in town, from the gamblers to the casinos to the mob—wants to know who these people are and how Lucky Peters analyzes their data to beat the spread."

"Maybe we should find out."

"Maybe we should. How do you know about the affair?"

"On her desktop there's a hand sanitizer and a colorful foam coaster that appears to have been painted by a child."

"Wow, you're truly amazing!"

"I know. It's called deductive reasoning."

"Uh huh. So you opened her computer, read her emails, and found out about her affair."

"Sounds so trivial when you put it that way. But yeah, lots of emails. Mostly sexual."

"Read me one."

"They're not impressive."

"Read one anyway. It's so intrusive! Makes me feel like we're doing something wrong."

"Unlike breaking and entering."

"You broke and entered. I'm just sitting here, living vicariously."

I click open her email account. "Okay, this one from last week is from Lucky. It says, 'I wish you'd come to Jamaica with me. I'd love to see you in a grass skirt.' And she says, 'They wear grass skirts in Hawaii, not Jamaica.' They argue about that a bit, then he says, 'We could hit that famous nude beach. I bet the natives have never seen an orange beaver before.' And she says, 'Especially with your initials on it!'"

Callie says, "Okay, I've heard enough."

"I tried to warn you."

We're silent a minute.

"I can't get it out of my mind," she says. "Orange beaver? His initials?"

"Me neither."

"She's supposed to be a doctor."

"I know."

"I keep picturing it," she says.

"Me too."

"You think she put all three initials, or just the two?" Callie says. "And if it's two, would it be JP or LP? And are the initials in hair? Or shaved out of it?"

"I'll ask her, if I get the chance."

"Please do," Callie says.

"I also found a small gift-wrapped box on her kitchen counter."

"Please tell me you opened it."

"Of course."

"Let me guess: a present for Lucky?"

"Cufflinks. An L and a P."

"Lucky Peters!" Callie says.

"Think about it," I say.

She's quiet a few seconds, then says, "Ah! Clever! Lucky and Phyllis!"

"He could wear them and his wife would never know."

"And is there a note?"

I smile. "There is."

"Please read it with passion in your voice."

"Your turn to get lucky!"

Callie laughs. "This is fun. Which tells you how sad my life is."

"Glad I could cheer you up."

"Is she cute?"

"Who, Phyllis? She's average." I think about it a few seconds, then say, "Above average."

"You think she went to Jamaica with him?"

"No. She sent an email telling him she hopes he's feeling better, and saying how awful to feel badly on vacation."

"What else have you learned?"

"You really want to know?"

"My choices are yes, or watch Celebrity Apprentice."

"Phyllis works all the time and she's lonely."

"Lonely? How do you know?"

"On her desktop there's a hand sanitizer and—"

"Move along, Donovan. It's getting old."

"She has only a couple of photographs on display. One is with her sister, the other with her parents. No messages on her answering machine."

"What's on her walls?"

"Art, mostly silk-screen."

"Of?"

"Faces."

"Famous ones?"

"Sad ones."

"You're breaking my heart," Callie says.

"What heart?"

"Good point. Don't forget to check her closet."

"Yes, Sensei."

"Women love to hide things in their closets."

"Right."

"And also in their underwear drawer."

"I'll be sure to check that one carefully."

"I've no doubt."

I end the call, walk down the hallway, enter the master bedroom. Phyllis's king size platform bed sits low and has a single mattress on a wood base, with no box spring. The bed is unmade on the right side, which tells me she slept alone last night. On the night stand are two prescription bottles: a statin drug and sleeping pills. After checking the date, I dump them out on the nightstand and count nineteen of each. If she started taking them on the fill date, there should be twenty. It's a fair assumption she's not coming home tonight, which works for me, since I need a place to stay.

According to her website, Phyllis's office opens at nine. I'll sleep on the left side of her bed tonight, shower, get up early, and break into her office at dawn. That'll give me time to search the place for anything that looks like a lethal, brain-melting device. Ideally, Phyllis will be the first to arrive, and we can settle this business without involving her staff.

In the nightstand drawer, behind a stack of *People* and US magazines, I find two boxes of condoms. One has been opened, and there are two packets missing, which tells me

31

Lucky appears to have gotten lucky at least twice.

The bedroom also has a chest of drawers and a small sitting area that faces a stucco fireplace that's never been used. The chest has five drawers, including a narrow one at the top, where she keeps her jewelry. I look through it and find nothing of significant value. I move from there to the bottom. The fifth drawer is pajamas, all bright colors, all cotton. Fourth drawer is socks in every size and color, and stockings. Third drawer is bras only. I count an even dozen, in various colors. Five are Ibex, Body by Victoria, 34-B, padded. She's also got a couple of jog bras in there.

Second drawer is filled with panties. I remove a few, and note they're all medium. Most are basic, but one is downright obscene. It has a circular hole cut out of the crotch. With red lips around it! I toss them back in the drawer, then think, no one has this many panties. I move my hands through them until I feel something.

It's my opinion that all women hide something special beneath their panties. But Dr. Phyllis Willis is hiding something lethal beneath hers.

4.

PHYLLIS KEEPS A single-action Smith and Wesson .22 automatic with three ten-round clips in her panty drawer, next to a small sex toy called a Pocket Rocket. I wouldn't pin high hopes on killing an intruder with a .22, but she's probably comfortable with the recoil and figures the sound would be enough to scare a guy away. Once he's gone, she probably breaks out the Pocket Rocket to celebrate.

I look at it a moment, then flip the switch and feel it buzz in my hand. Noting briefly that the buzz is more pleasant than the one in my head, I think about where the device has been. I toss it back in the drawer, march into her bathroom, and thoroughly wash my hands before getting back to business.

The clothes hanging in Phyllis's closet tell me she's a size eight. She has an abundance of cocktail dresses and business suits, which makes sense for a plastic surgeon who has to attend fundraisers and cocktail parties and hobnob with the rich and famous. For the most part, her clothes, shoes and handbags are basic, tasteful, and functional, and I find nothing extravagant here. I check through the sweaters, the hat boxes and other items on her shelves. I stand there, looking around the closet, wondering if I'm missing anything. I think about the Pocket Rocket again, and call Doc Howard.

"What about a Pocket Rocket?"

"Donovan, check your watch."

I do. "So?"

"So I'm in Virginia. Remember?"

"Well, I've never met Virginia. But if you're in her, I'm sure she's special."

"Funny."

"This controller thing you mentioned. Would it fit in a Pocket Rocket?"

"What's a Pocket Rocket?"

"A woman's vibrator. A sex toy."

"Donovan, I'm an old man. Maybe you should just shoot me and get it over with."

"Maybe I will."

He sighs. "I don't know the dimensions of your sex toy or the controller device. I don't even know if there is a controller device. Why don't you take the thing apart and see?"

"I've got sort of a germ thing if I don't know the person."

"Can I go back to bed now?"

I hang up. Five minutes later, the Pocket Rocket is in pieces on Phyllis's bathroom counter. I'm not sure what I'm looking for, but there doesn't seem to be anything on the counter that could liquefy my brains. After three attempts, I give up trying to put it back together. I take the pieces back to her pajama drawer and toss them in. Then I go to Phyllis's computer, call Lou Kelly, and give him access to Phyllis's computer so his geeks can make a remote copy of everything that's on it. That done, I tell Lou to run an exhaustive search on Jim "Lucky" Peters. Then I remove the hard drive and put it on the kitchen counter so I won't forget to take it with me in the morning.

After inspecting Phyllis's house and garage from top to bottom, I check her refrigerator and pantry for something to cook. She's poorly stocked, but I find some Kalamata olive halves, walnuts, bow-tie pasta, and parmesan cheese. While the salted water for the pasta heats up, I stir-fry the olives and walnuts in olive oil, grind some pepper into it, and let it simmer on low. When the water reaches a boil, I pour in the pasta, stir it, then put a lid on the pan and remove it from the heat for 11 minutes, like the package says. Then I drain it, put it back in the pan, and stir in the olive mixture, and grate some parmesan cheese over it.

I could have done something fancier, but this hit the spot, and anyway, I've got an early day tomorrow.

Just before falling asleep in Phyllis's bed, I think about everything I've seen and found in her house. And that gives me an idea. I don't know why this seems like a good idea, but something in my head tells me what I'm about to do could come in handy.

I get up and remove a single condom from Phyllis's condom drawer, and put it in the little box with the cufflinks she planned to give Lucky. Then I re-wrap the present, and put it on the kitchen counter next to the hard drive.

5.

MONDAY MORNING, SEVEN-THIRTY.

I've been at PhySpa, Phyllis's day spa and plastic surgery center for more than two hours, but couldn't find the device. I'm disappointed Phyllis hasn't arrived yet. I hear someone unlock the front door, so I sneak out the back and head for the nearest coffee shop. I don't know who entered, but it wasn't Phyllis, because her name is on the only parking space behind the building, and she would have used that entrance.

After a coffee and bathroom stop, it's eight a.m., and I'm surprised to see several cars parked in front of PhySpa. When I enter the waiting room, the receptionist asks if she can help me.

The sign on the front desk tells me her name.

"Hi Shelby."

"Hello," she says, brightly.

I lean in close and say, "I wonder if I could speak to Dr. Willis for a quick minute about something personal."

She frowns. He doesn't look like a salesman, Shelby's thinking. But she's not sure.

"Your name, please?"

"Connor Payne."

"I'll check."

When she does, something in Shelby's facial expression gives me the distinct impression Phyllis Willis is less than thrilled I'm in her lobby. Shelby says, "Yes, certainly," and places the phone carefully in its cradle before saying, "I'm sorry, Mr. Payne, but Dr. Willis is in the middle of a procedure."

I smile sweetly and say, "Shelby."

"Yes sir?"

"Call her again. Tell her if she's not out here in two minutes, I'm coming for her."

She looks like she's about to say something, but changes her mind and repeats my message to Phyllis. I wait a minute, then feel a buzzing in my brain that tells me someone in the office—probably Phyllis—is trying to enter the kill code. The buzzing hurts ten times worse than the one I felt on Saturday night.

Son of a bitch!

I grab both sides of my head and stagger backward.

Shelby jumps to her feet. "Sir! Are you okay?"

The buzzing stops. I shake my head.

"Sir?"

"I'm okay, thanks."

"Are you sure?"

"Positive."

And I am, until—Shit!

She's doing it again!

When the buzzing stops I take a few seconds to regain my equilibrium. Then I paralyze Shelby with a throat strike before killing her quickly. I kiss her forehead before lowering her carefully to the floor.

I know what you're thinking: Shelby would rather be alive than kissed by her killer. I agree. She doesn't deserve this, and it sucks. But I'm under attack, and she controls the phones and can identify me.

I lock the front door, then move through Phyllis's office

37

like clap through a whorehouse.

I open one door after another. Most of the rooms are empty, but I manage to find and kill a spa attendant, a masseuse, and the face-down woman he's working on. I didn't catch any of their names. I don't enjoy killing innocent people, but my situation is critical. I had hoped to meet with Phyllis in private, but she tried to kill me instead. And might still accomplish it, since I don't know how the device works. If I had the luxury of time, these people would still be alive.

But when Phyllis made her move, I had to make mine.

Within a minute, it's just me and Phyllis, who I find cowering on the floor of her bathroom.

She'd been on her cell phone.

"Who were you talking to, Phyllis?"

"N-No one," she says.

I slap the right side of her face with the palm of my hand, and then the left side with the back of my hand, hard enough to open a small gash on both corners of her mouth. The way the blood trickles out makes her mouth look like the Joker in *Batman*. Except she's not smiling.

I grab her cell phone and tap the button marked "Recent." The name "Lucky" appears. I slip her phone into my pocket, figuring to check her caller list later.

"Who's Lucky?"

"N-No one."

She sees me looking at the controller in her lap, the one that looks like a fancy wristwatch. The one she used to punch in the code a few minutes ago. The code she thought would kill me.

"Looosy?" I say in my best Ricky Ricardo voice. "You've got some 'splainin' to do!"

6.

"THERE'S SOME SORT of device that can reprogram the chip in my brain," I say.

Phyllis's face takes on a look of extreme sadness. She knows I'm a stone killer, and knows I'm aware she tried to kill me moments ago. She moves her lips, trying to form words. The effort makes her mouth look like that of a small bird, straining upward, waiting for its mother to drop a bit of worm down its throat.

"Phyllis, I need you to focus. I'm not talking about the unit you used to try to kill me just now. I'm talking about a master device that can override these wrist units."

"Y-yes. There is one."

"And what does it look like?"

"It's v-very small."

"And what does it look like?"

"Like the t-tip of a..." She pauses, trying to come up with a name. Gives up and says, "a computer memory thing."

I pull out my phone, press the button that speed-dials Lou's number.

"I've got lots of stuff on the gambler," Lou says. "But more to come. And we're still digging through the doctor's files from when you linked her computer to ours last night. You want what I've got so far?"

"Not yet. I do have a question, though."

"Shoot."

"What's a computer memory thing?"

Lou pauses. "Is this a riddle?"

"Not on purpose."

I need Lou's help, but I don't want him to know there's a chip in my brain that can kill me. Lou and I are close, but since he tried to murder me recently, I'd prefer to keep a few secrets from him. I say, "I'm with a woman who's trying to think of what you call the small tip of a computer memory thing."

"What's the shape?" Lou says.

I repeat the question to Phyllis and she stammers out it's a rectangle, and people stick it into the side of their computers.

"Into the USB port?" Lou asks.

I ask Phyllis. She nods.

"Yes," I tell Lou. "It fits into the USB port."

"She's talking about a flash drive," Lou says. "Also known as a memory stick, finger stick, pen drive, disk-on-key, jump drive—"

"Got it," I say. "Thanks."

It takes a minute, but I eventually get Phyllis to explain that the master device resembles the metal tip of a flash drive, except that it's ceramic, and half the size.

"And is it silver?" I ask.

"Wh-White."

"Where is it?"

"I-I don't have it."

"Is it in this office?"

"N-No. I sw-swear."

She's trembling, and seems very small and frail. Much smaller than the clothes in her closet would indicate. Maybe it's because she's curled up in a fetal position. She's crying, and her mascara is running and her mouth is bleeding, and her hair's a coffee-colored mess.

"Your hair's not orange," I say.

"Wh-what?"

"You dyed your sweet spot orange?" I say.

She gives me a confused look. "My wh-what?"

"I was trying not to be vulgar. Your bush. You dyed it orange? Intentionally?"

She follows my gaze and modestly covers her lap with her hands.

"Have you given it to someone?"

"Excuse me?"

"The device."

Phyllis nods.

"Who?"

"Mrs. Peters."

I pause. "Lucky's wife?"

She nods.

"No shit?"

She shakes her head.

Before I kill her I say, "I don't mean to embarrass you, but I promised my friend I'd ask you something."

7.

"THE INITIALS LP were shaved out of her bush," I say to Callie.

"Did you verify that personally?"

"No. I trusted her."

"Is she in heaven now?"

"With Saint Peter, you mean? Instead of Lucky Peters?"

"Hard to think of Lucky Peters as a saint."

"What else do you know about him?"

"He's seeking investors."

"For what?"

"He wants to build a sports book facility. Vegas Moon, he calls it."

"Vegas Moon?"

"Biggest Sports Book under the Sun. That's his slogan."

"Makes sense. About him owning a sports book."

"Casinos aren't happy about it."

"I suppose not. You know anything about his wife?"

"Nope. Just that she's a young trophy. He keeps her out of the public eye, for the most part."

"What does he look like?"

"Lucky? Yucky."

"Can you be more specific?"

"Charles Manson in a Stetson."

"That's a happy thought," I say. Then add, "Are you still home?"

"What do you need?"

"A shower, and the suit I left there."

"Got a date?"

"I'm hopeful."

"Anyone I know?"

"Gwen."

"Who's that?"

"Lucky's wife."

"Does she know you're coming?"

"Not yet."

8.

ONE OF THE great things about having unlimited financial and government resources is the ability to get what you need in a short period of time. Thirty minutes after telling Lou I need an off-the-books police car and a van with no windows in back, driven by a couple of trustworthy guys, they arrive at the parking area behind Callie's condo. In the meantime, I drag Shelby out of the front office so no one will look through the glass door and see a dead receptionist. Then I dig the car keys out of her purse, locate her car, and drive it halfway to Callie's. I jog the rest of the way, shower at Callie's, and change into the suit I'd brought.

My plan is to drive the cop car to Lucky's house, park it near the front door, pose as a cop investigating a major breach of national security. I'll tell Gwen that Phyllis has implicated her in the theft of stolen corporate property, namely the device. With any luck, I'll scare her into giving it back. If she doesn't, I'll have to intensify the questioning. I tell the guys to follow me in the panel van and use it to block Lucky's driveway after I enter.

So that's the plan.

Unfortunately, when I get there, Lucky's house is a fortress.

Worse, it's crawling with cops.

I drive past his house, suddenly very aware I'm driving an unauthorized police car. I need to ditch it, and quickly. I call the guys in the van and tell them there's been a change in plans and we're heading to the airport. I'll put the cop car in long-term parking, and have the guys drive me back to Callie's.

I end the call and start another one.

"What happened?" Callie says.

I tell her. Then say, "Why would the cops be at Lucky's house?"

"You think they found Phyllis already?"

"By now? Sure. But why would they race to Lucky's house? Does everyone in town know about the affair?"

"I wouldn't think so."

"We'll figure it out. Can I crash at your condo awhile?"

"I'll set an extra place at the table for lunch."

"You're cooking?"

"Yup."

"Wow, you are bored."

When I get there I learn Callie's idea of cooking means chopping lettuce, hard-boiled eggs and assorted veggies for a salad.

"Can you see if I have what you need to make a salad dressing?" she says.

"Got extra virgin olive oil?"

"Yup."

"Some sort of vinegar?"

"Balsamic?"

"Then we're good."

Turns out her pantry is a treasure trove for a vinaigrette meister like me. I find shallots, garlic, honey, and an orange. Her spice cabinet yields mustard, sugar, salt, ground white pepper, celery seed. I mince a couple of shallots and a bit of garlic, grate a little orange peel, and blend these with the other ingredients, and set the mixture on the counter so the flavors can blend.

"The oil and vinegar will separate before we eat the salad," she says.

"No they won't."

"Ever heard the expression oil and vinegar don't mix?"

"I think you mean oil and water."

"That's the lesser-known expression, as any cook will tell you."

"You're a cook now?"

"Well, I didn't run a bed and breakfast in Florida and hunt squirrels in the attic like that guy in the novel."

"Funny."

"But it doesn't change things. The oil and vinegar will separate."

"I added some honey."

"So?"

"It sustains the emulsion."

She cocks her head at me. "Do you ever listen to yourself talk?"

"No. That's your job."

She pulls the cover off the blender, pokes her index finger into the vinaigrette, licks it.

"Fuck the salad," she says.

"Excuse me?"

"I could make a meal out of this. Why's it so good?"

"Why wouldn't it be?"

Callie opens her silverware drawer, takes out a spoon, dips it in the mixture, puts the spoon in her mouth, swallows. Then licks the spoon.

Sees me staring at her mouth.

"What?" she says.

"Have you ever heard of a Pocket Rocket?"

She gives me a curious look, then says, "You asshole!"

"Huh?"

"You were fantasizing about me. Again."

"What makes you think—"

"Sexually."

"Well…"

"It's just a mouth, Donovan. Everyone's got one."

"Not like yours."

She shakes her head. "Not gonna happen."

"Why not?"

She smiles. "What difference does it make?"

I shrug.

She dips her spoon into the dressing again, puts it up to her mouth. But this time, before tasting it, she blocks her mouth from my view with her other hand. Then she winks.

"You know I love you," I say.

"How could you not?"

My cell phone starts vibrating.

"I've made vinaigrette a dozen times," she says.

"So?"

"It never turns out like this."

"The ratio of oil to vinegar is everything."

My phone vibrates again. I look at the caller ID.

"Tell me," Callie says.

"Three parts oil to one part vinegar."

I answer the phone.

It's Carmine "The Chin" Porrello, telling me about a call he got from Lucky Peters, who'd been looking for a hit man. I thank him, ask if Lucky's banging anyone besides his wife. Carmine doesn't know her name off hand, but yeah, some plastic surgeon. He's got photos.

"Sex photos?"

Callie arches an eyebrow at me.

Carmine says, "Nah. Just the two of 'em together. Dinner shit. Nothin' I can use. Not yet."

Then I call Lou and tell him to have his geek squad access Lucky's medical records at the hospital in Kingston.

"You want to hold while I get that for you?" Lou says.

"It's that easy?"

"I should probably say no, and charge you extra. But yeah, it's that easy."

I cover the mouthpiece and say to Callie, "You never answered me about the Pocket Rocket."

"Nor will I," she says. "Ever."

I frown. "Why not?"

"If I tell you about our sex life, you'll never look at me and Eva the same way again."

"And that's a bad thing?"

"Yup."

"Why?"

She gives me an exasperated look, rolls her eyes. Then says, "You make such a big deal out of sex."

"Who doesn't?"

Lou gets back on the phone, tells me about Dr. Gayle and the colonoscopy. Then says, "Lucky's meeting investors this week. Putting together an offering for a sports betting parlor."

"Vegas Moon, right?"

"Right. You want what I've got?"

"I'll have to call you back. I've got another call coming in."

I terminate Lou's call, click the incoming one.

It's Lucky Peters, offering me a job.

9.

"LET ME GET this straight," Callie says. "Lucky Peters is hiring you to protect him from Connor Payne?"

"Correct."

"And you're Connor Payne."

"That's right."

"That's what I call a cushy job."

"The best part, I get access to his house, his business, and his weirdos."

"You thinking about stealing his ideas?"

"No."

"Taking over his business?"

"No."

"Running a scam?"

"Hadn't thought about it."

"Then why do you care about his business?"

"I keep thinking there's one person in the world who could beat Lucky Peters at his own game."

"Who's that?"

"Sam Case."

Callie pauses. "You'd go into business with Sam?"

"I can't imagine it, but who knows. It's just a *Rain Man* idea at this point."

"You're fascinated by the lifestyle."

"A little."

"Donovan, trust me. This town will eat you up. They don't play fair."

"So I've heard. But betting is all about understanding the odds of probability. If Lucky's winning all the time, he knows how to calibrate the point spread. He's probably got a bunch of people betting one side of the wager, helping him improve the odds. When he feels the number's right, he has another bunch bet big money on the other side."

"Of course. That's public knowledge. He admits to manipulating the odds."

"Isn't that illegal?"

"Not according to the grand jury. He's been indicted twice."

"And?"

"They tossed it out both times."

"Don't you think Sam could calculate the odds better than Lucky?"

"He's got the mind for it, but no, I don't think so."

"Why not?"

"Sam doesn't know shit about sports."

I frown. "That can't be true."

Callie gives me a dirty look. "I dated him for a month, remember?"

"Right. Sorry."

She shakes her head in disgust. "I had sex with him!"

"Once. As I recall, you came out of it quite wealthy."

"Still."

I say, "The whole gambling thing is fascinating, but I took the job so I could meet Gwen."

"You plan to charm her into giving you the device?"

"If I have access to the house, I'll find the device."

"When do you start?"

"Right after lunch."

"Lucky wants you to what, watch Gwen?"

"Yeah. I'm to introduce myself to Gwen, keep an eye on her till he gets back, late tonight. He wants me and Gwen to pick him up at the airport. I'm not supposed to let her out of my sight."

"How convenient."

"I know. Talk about things falling into place."

"You want me to slip into his house when you go to the airport? Help you find the device?"

"I might. Let me get a feel for his security first."

"Oh, please."

"I know you can get past whatever he's got in place, but I want to make it easy for you."

She shrugs.

I'm quiet for several minutes. Callie waits, knowing I'm working an angle. Finally, I look up at her and smile.

"You've got a plan," she says.

"A contingency plan."

"And?"

"And if we need it, you're going to love it!"

"Goody. Let's eat."

10.

BEFORE WE TUCK into our salads, I call a car rental agency and tell them to pick me up at twelve-fifteen, which gives me forty-five minutes. When I go down the elevator, the driver's waiting for me in the lobby. I sign the paperwork, ask if he needs a ride back to the lot. He does, so I take him, then drive out to Lucky's house for the second time in three hours.

This time when I approach, there are no cop cars. There are two muscleheads working the gate, however, and I have to show them my ID and give a password before entering. The password is the name of Lucky's doctor in Jamaica, Dr. Gayle. Satisfied with the answer, the gate goons open the gates. I drive through, and down the long driveway, and park by the turnaround. From there I walk to the front door, climb the four stone steps, and stare at the twelve-foot-high, four-inch-thick, mahogany doors, until one of them slowly opens.

Gwen is very young, and stunning.

Not Callie Carpenter stunning, or even supermodel stunning. But Gwen would be right at home with any of the troubled TV and movie starlets I've seen on the news. The ones who are in and out of court, and rehab, and who always show their naughty bits when entering or exiting limos. She has that same bored, pouty look that tells men she knows what she wants, and has the currency to get it.

What she doesn't look like is a wife.

Gwen holds out her hand, introduces herself. I take it, and tell her who I am. When we end the handshake, she stands aside so I can enter. When I do, she closes the door behind me, locks it and says, "He's got tits, you know."

"Excuse me?"

I turn to face her. She's wearing gray sweatpants and a pink T-shirt upon which is printed: TREAT ME! RIGHT. Except that the first two letters and the last five are printed in black, while the rest are in red.

If she and Lucky break up, if her T-shirt is any indication, I can picture Gwen babysitting for Charlie Sheen.

"Boobs. Hooters. Breasts. You know, tits," she says, cupping her ample breasts.

"I know what they are," I say. "I'm just not sure what you're saying. About Lucky."

She circles around me, and starts walking.

I'm supposed to follow.

Not that I mind following. She's got an athletic body that looks just as good from this angle as it does from the front. It doesn't take long for my eyes to adjust to the hypnotic sway of her backside, as she moves down the hallway. On a scale of one to ten, I give her a two for attitude, and a nine-point-five for looks.

Sometimes I tell Lou Kelly or my daughter, Kimberly, about the people I run across, and they say, "Is every woman you meet drop-dead gorgeous?" I'm sure it seems that way, because I do encounter an outsized number of beautiful women in my line of work. It makes sense that I would, since most of my male clients are exceptionally wealthy, and can afford to support such women. And the women assassins I know, with the exception of Carla Mutato, were recruited primarily for their looks, and trained afterward. At the same time, my business often takes me to the opposite end of the spectrum, where I deal with dead-eyed killers, wide-eyed thieves, junkies, hardened criminals, broken-nosed bodyguards, nasty-assed pimps, broken-down whores, scar-faced mob enforcers, and a wide assortment of others who, together, comprise the very dregs of humanity. So it's either roses or thorns for me. Because not many average-looking people play in my park.

"You've got great hair," I say.

"Thanks."

She does have great hair. It's thick and lustrous, and a rich mahogany brown in color, with subtle highlights at the ends. Frosted would be too much. What she's done is unique, and to me, classy.

Gwen motions me to sit at the kitchen table. I do. She brings two beers from the fridge, hands me one. "Coors okay?"

I shrug, and twist off the top. She does the same, then holds her bottle next to mine, so we can toast. When that's done, she smiles and says, "Lucky has implants. 34-C's."

"No way!"

She laughs. "Swear to God!"

"Why?"

"He bet the wrong team in the Super Bowl. I mean, his team won, but they didn't beat the spread. The guy who won offered him a cash option, but Lucky chose the boob job."

"The guy's worth millions. Why would he do that?"

"'Cause he's cheaper than shit."

I know what this is all about. She's bullshitting me, trying to see how gullible I am. Then she says, "Wanna see a picture?"

"Of?"

"Lucky's boobs."

Maybe she isn't bullshitting me. I shrug. "Why not?"

54

She leaves the room a minute, comes back holding a photo, shows it to me. Callie's right about his looks. From the neck up, he's scary. But the tits are spectacular.

"Who did the surgery?"

"Phyllis Willis."

I must have glanced at Gwen's chest without thinking, because she says, "Yeah, she did mine, too."

"Well, if they're as nice as these…"

"They're better."

"Alrighty then."

11.

"SHE'S DEAD, YOU know," Gwen says, after polishing off her second beer.

"Who?"

"Phyllis Willis."

"The plastic surgeon?"

Gwen nods. "She was murdered. And four people in her office. It's all over the news."

"When did it happen?"

"Early this morning. The police were here for, like, an hour."

"Why here?"

"She wrote a message on the bottom side of the toilet lid with her lipstick. When the detective went in there to pee, he lifted the lid and saw the message."

I shake my head. Phyllis kicked my ass with that one. I must be slipping.

"What did the message say?"

"Connor Payne did this. Lucky and Gwen Peters are next."

"Why you?"

"That's what the police wanted to know."

"And you said?"

"I told them I never heard of Connor Payne." She looks at me carefully. "But you have, haven't you." A statement, not a question.

"I have."

"Is he a depraved maniac?"

"Some people think so."

"But you could kill him?"

"I could."

She gets up to fetch another beer from the fridge. "Want one?"

"I'm good."

"You don't look like a hit man," Gwen says.

"What do I look like?"

"Some actor. Can't remember his name. One of the handsome ones. You probably get that a lot."

"I do, actually. But thanks."

"It's not a compliment."

"No?"

"Anyone can have good looks. What counts is money."

"Right."

"And power."

"Yup."

"And fame."

"Lucky's got those things," I say.

"He does. But he's not powerful."

"No?"

"Not like you."

We look at each other a minute, then she says, "Speaking of hit men, you want a hit, man?" She grins at her joke.

"I don't."

She stares at me the way she might look at a talking dog.

"Everyone snorts," she says.

"Not me."

"Shit," she says. "You're what my mother would call a square."

"How old's your mother?" I say.

She laughs. "You don't want to know."

She's right. I don't.

Then she says, "You want to see my cock?"

12.

"EXCUSE ME?"

She grins. "My rooster. Where was your mind just now, gutter man?"

"You've got a rooster? Here?"

"I do. Wanna see it?"

"What's his name?"

Without a hint of smile, she says, "Dick."

"Your rooster's name is Dick."

She giggles. "You love it, right?"

I shrug. What do I care what she named the damn bird?

"Ask me," she says.

"Ask you what?"

"If you can see it."

I was about to accuse her of being childish. Then again, she appears to be twenty. Of course, my new girlfriend, Miranda the hooker, is also twenty. But she's a gifted student, living in Brooklyn, working toward her Master's in Counseling Psychology at NYU. I wonder if twenty years old in Brooklyn is like dog's years compared to Vegas.

Gwen stands. "If you ask me nicely to see it, I'll give you a kiss."

"Are you flirting with me?"

"Of course!"

I smile. "In that case, please show me your cock!"

She walks around the table, bends down, kisses my cheek.

"Come," she says, taking my hand.

I stand and allow her to lead me through a stone arch and down a long, marble hall.

"Nice house," I say.

"Twelve thousand square feet," she says.

"How many live here?"

"Me and Dick, and Lucky."

"Anyone else ever come inside?"

"You didn't just say that."

"Funny. But seriously."

"You're awfully nosey."

"I'm the bodyguard."

"Tina the housekeeper, and sometimes Maddie."

We stop. She opens a door and says, "This is the theater room. Nice, huh?"

"It certainly is. Who's Maddie?"

"Maddie's my girlfriend."

"When you say 'girlfriend'…"

"She and I have sex, while Lucky watches."

"Does she happen to be here today?" I ask.

"Aren't you the eager beaver?" she says.

"I was just taking inventory."

"Of course you were." She closes the theater room door, and leads me to the next one. "This goes to the garage, home of Dick the rooster."

She opens the door and waits for me to enter.

"After you," I say.

"Aren't you the gentleman!"

Not really. I was afraid if the rooster was running around loose, it might fly up and attack me. If one of us has to take a cock to the face, I'd prefer it was her.

13.

THERE'S NO NEED to worry about Dick. He's locked in a
giant cage that's six feet high, four feet deep, and takes up half
the wall.

"Beautiful, isn't he!" she says, practically breathlessly.

I don't know much about roosters, but this one is probably
as handsome and clean as they get. He's white, with a giant,
black plume of a tail, and his head and neck sport that red
rooster skin thing they all have that looks like a punk rocker's
spiked hair above the beak, and a giant set of nuts below. It's
a generally nasty look. Freaky, up close.

"He's quite a specimen," I proclaim, for lack of anything
better to say.

"While we're here," Gwen says, "we ought to go ahead and
walk him."

"Walk him?"

She looks into my eyes. "Unless you think it's too
dangerous."

I look into hers. They're mud-brown, but far prettier than
that sounds. "We'll be fine," I say.

Her smile is so sudden and radiant, it takes me by surprise.

"What?" I say.

"You're really tough, aren't you? I mean, you're the real
deal."

"You think?"

Gwen launches a punch to my face, which I easily catch in my hand. She smiles and says, "I know it."

She crosses the floor to a small sink, turns on the water, and lets it run long enough to warm. Next, she gets a cotton ball from a container and wets it with warm water. She removes the bird from the cage, holds it upside down and starts stroking it with the cotton ball.

"What are you doing?"

"Dick hasn't peed today."

"So?"

"If you rub a warm, moist cotton ball on his genitals, it stimulates him to pee."

I think about telling her I haven't peed since early this morning.

Gwen waits a moment, then frowns.

"Maybe the walk will help him pee," she says. She fits him with a harness and attaches a leash to it. Then she pops the garage door open, and starts to leave.

"Shouldn't we lock the door?" I say.

"Probably. Punch in 5197, then hit Enter."

I do as instructed, and we stroll down the driveway, walking her rooster.

"You know what I call this?" she says.

"The cock walk?"

Gwen smiles. "How'd you know?"

"Nothing else would be quite right."

"Exactly."

It takes much longer than I would have thought to walk a rooster to the end of the driveway. As we approach the gates, the gate goons puff themselves up to impress her. But Gwen doesn't seem to notice, or at least pretends not to. We pass by them, stand on the road a few minutes, then turn around and head back to the garage.

"Does he crow every morning at dawn?" I ask.

"Do you kill someone every morning at dawn?" she says, testily.

I think briefly about the five I killed this morning, but decide hers is a rhetorical question.

"Did I offend you by asking that?" I say.

"It's just a stupid question."

"Don't roosters crow in the mornings?"

"No more than any other time. It's a myth."

"You sure about that?"

"Quite."

We walk some more. Then I say, "What's that red stuff on his head and neck?"

"Wattles and comb."

"And the red-and-white part?"

"His earlobes. You don't know much about roosters, do you, Mr. Creed?"

She could have said cocks, for shock value. But something tells me we've moved past that now.

"Please. Call me Donovan."

She stops short.

"What's wrong?" I ask.

She turns and nods toward the two muscleheads guarding the gate. "Could you take them down without a gun?"

I don't even look up. "Yes."

"Both of them? At the same time?"

"I doubt one would stand still while I kill the other."

We start walking again, only now she's walking much closer to me.

63

14.

"HOW MUCH DO you charge?"

"What, to guard Lucky?"

We're back in the kitchen. It's four p.m. Gwen has just polished off beer number four.

"To kill someone."

"Depends on the job."

"In general."

"Each job is different."

We're sitting across the table from each other. Gwen is twisting her hair with her thumb and index finger. She's not drunk, but not sober, either. She's in that middle zone, where endless possibilities reside. Tipsy enough to exude sensuality, but sober enough to know what she's doing. And saying.

"So," she says. "If I hired you to kill one of the guards out front, what would it cost me?"

"Nothing."

She perks up. "What do you mean?"

"I'm on the clock. I'd kill them both for free, if they tried to hurt you or Lucky."

"Oh," she says. Then says, "But say they weren't trying to hurt us. Say I just wanted one of them dead?"

"I'd need a reason," I say.

"I thought hit men killed 'cause it's their job."

"We kill for lots of reasons. I'm one of those who never

used to ask questions."

"And now you do?"

"Depends on the client."

"I don't understand."

"You're what, twenty years old?"

"Yes."

"Well, if you were twice that, I probably wouldn't need a reason."

Her eyes widen just enough to show I offended her. But not too much.

"Are you saying I'm not mature enough to make that decision?"

"That's what I'm saying."

"But if I had a good reason?"

"I'd do it."

She nods. "For how much?"

"Those guys at the gate?"

"They're pretty tough," she says. "Lucky wouldn't have hired them if they weren't."

I nod. "Ten."

"Ten thousand?"

"No. Cents."

Gwen's smile blooms before my eyes, and spreads across her face.

She says, "Would you be offended if I gave you a real kiss right now?"

"You mean here, at the table?"

"For now."

"What about Lucky?"

"He'll have to wait for his kiss."

"The answer is no."

Her smile fades. "Why not?"

"I meant no, I wouldn't be offended."

She smiles again, climbs into the chair next to mine, puts her arms around me, and gives me a long, slow, hot-breathed kiss. When she pulls away, her face is flushed. She stands and says, "That was nice, Donovan."

"Nicer for me, I expect."

"Maybe," she says. "And maybe not."

With that, she turns toward the opposite hall.

"Where are you off to?" I ask.

She stops, turns around. "My bedroom."

"A nap?"

"Eventually. First, I'm going to lock the door, remove my clothes, climb into bed, and, um...think...about what just happened."

"Wow! I hate to miss that!"

She smiles. "Disregard any gasps you might hear."

"Maybe you should leave the door unlocked. You know, in case you need help."

"The area I plan to focus on is very small. I think I can handle it myself."

This time when she turns, she keeps walking until she's out of view. A moment later, I hear a door close. I take a deep breath, and let it out slowly.

Then I start searching the house.

15.

I DON'T SEE GWEN again till 8:15 p.m., when she enters the kitchen, dressed to kill.

"Wow!"

"The one word a woman loves to hear when she dresses up," she says.

"Again, then. Wow!" And I meant it.

"Zip me up in the back?" she says sweetly, turning away from me.

She's wearing a simple black sweater with the sleeves rolled up to just above the elbows, tucked into a black, pleated skirt, and fire-engine-red boots with black heels that have rhinestone strips attached over the toe, and above the upper ankle. The boots stop mid-calf, leaving plenty of leg showing. I move behind her and pull the material toward me enough to peek down her back.

"You cad!" she says.

"That word is way too old for you," I say.

"Nevertheless, it applies."

"How so?"

"Come on, Donovan. We both know you were checking to see if I had panties on."

"Guilty. Sorry."

"That's all right. I'd be disappointed if you didn't want to see."

"Why?"

"It's a girl thing. You wouldn't understand."

"I understand enough to know it isn't easy matching panties to those boots."

She spins around and finds herself quite close to me.

"You'll have to back away quickly," Gwen says, "or I'll wind up smearing my lipstick."

I take a couple of steps back, reluctantly. I don't know what it is about this young woman that's getting to me. Yes, she's beautiful. Enticing. But there's more. She's incredibly sensual, in a bad girl sort of way. Not "hooker sensual," or "prison bad." More like: colleg-girl-who's-fucking-her-dad's-business-partner bad. She heads to the fridge to get one last beer before we leave for the airport.

"Want one?"

"Nope."

"Don't drink much, do you."

"I'm a bourbon guy."

"You should've said. Would you like one now?"

"Maybe later."

Gwen twists the top off and takes a long swallow. When she looks back at me, I ask, "How well did you know Phyllis?"

"Phyllis the Willis?" She shrugs. "Phyllis did some work on me. Boobs, chemical peel, laser hair removal. Mostly I spent time at the spa. I mean, we spoke, but she didn't like me."

"Are you sure?"

"Positive."

"Because?"

"I think it's because she was fucking Lucky."

"You think?"

"I don't know for sure. But it wouldn't surprise me."

"Why not?"

"She seriously didn't like me. Always made me feel uncomfortable. I hate to say it, but I'm glad she's dead."

"Because she didn't like you?"

"Because they were always together. She was on the board of that company, Ropic Industries, and Lucky's the major stockholder."

"Is the stock doing well?"

"How the fuck should I know?"

I suddenly hear something, and jump to the side of the kitchen door.

"What?" Gwen says.

"Someone's coming in the back. Duck behind the counter!"

I crouch, ready to strike.

"Relax, killer. It's Tina."

Turns out it is Tina, the housekeeper, returning from wherever she'd been all afternoon. Gwen introduces us and tells her which bedroom I'll be camping in tonight. Tina immediately grabs some sheets from the laundry room and heads toward the bedroom that's situated between Gwen's bedroom and the kitchen.

Gwen says, "Lucky's such a jerk."

"What do you mean?"

"Tina's usually gone by five. But her daughter had an operation today, so naturally she wanted to be at the hospital with her. Lucky said fine, but she'd have to work late to make up for it."

"Wow."

"Great guy, right?"

While Gwen had been napping and showering, I searched every room on this side of the house, trying to find the device. And came up with nothing. While she was getting dressed, I called Lou Kelly, who told me that Lucky's twenty million dollar investment in Ropic Industries was practically worthless. According to the terms of his stockholder purchase petition, he can't sell his shares for several months. By then, the company will be bankrupt. This, according to one of Lou's SEC buddies who said they're about to publicly announce a full-scale investigation of Ropic's accounting practices.

I don't care about Lucky's financial problems, I just want the device. After talking to Lou, I walked through the rooms one last time, to see if I'd overlooked something obvious.

I hadn't.

If a professional had hidden the device, I'd need a week to conduct a proper search. But Gwen's a civilian, and I'd bet serious coin she hasn't hidden it in the rooms I've searched. Which leaves Lucky's office, their bedroom, bath, and closet.

"I should check out your bedroom," I say. "For security reasons."

"You'll have to wait till Lucky gets home."

"Why?"

"His command center adjoins it."

"Command center?"

"It's where he makes the magic. No one's allowed in there."

"Not even you?" I say.

"Not even."

16.

"DONOVAN?" GWEN SAYS.

"Yes?"

"Don't pay any attention to how I act when Lucky gets here."

"What do you mean?"

"I'll probably be all over him."

"Okay."

"But it's an act."

"I'm sorry."

"Don't be. It's a good life."

"Is it?"

"When I'm not bored out of my skull."

While waiting, I take a minute to wonder why pretty girls are always bored at home.

Soon she says, "Here he comes. In the cowboy hat."

"They're all wearing cowboy hats."

"He's the one looks stupid in it."

"You don't mean…"

"I do. That Jesus freak in the sandals? Wearing the cowboy hat?"

"That's Lucky?"

"In the pock-marked flesh."

He looks worse in person than he did in his photo.

Thirty minutes later the three of us are in my car, heading

toward PhySpa. Lucky's riding shotgun, Gwen's sitting behind him.

Gwen says, "When we get to the next intersection, turn right."

"We don't have time for that," Lucky says.

"I want Mr. Creed to see what he's protecting."

"He's protecting us."

"C'mon, Lucky, it'll only take a second."

He sighs. "Fine."

I take the next right a half-block, turn left into a paved entrance that ends twenty feet into the vacant lot.

"Put your brights on," Gwen says.

I do. The extra wattage illuminates a large sign, thirty yards in front of us. It says, Future Home of Vegas Moon! Underneath that, in smaller script, are the words Greatest Sports Book under the Sun!

"This is the most valuable vacant lot in all of Las Vegas," she says.

"I don't doubt it."

"And it's going to be named after me."

"Shut up, Gwen," Lucky says.

"I'm just proud, is all."

It's not my business to ask what she means about the name, so I say, "Well, it's a great piece of land."

"That's where I'll be buried someday," she says.

"Oh Jeez," Lucky says. "Not this again."

"I'm going to be buried there someday," she says. "And you have to respect my dying wish. If I die before you open the sports book, I want you to bury me right smack under the sign."

"I will," Lucky says. "Sooner, instead of later. If you don't shut the fuck up."

I think it's an odd thing for her to say. I seriously doubt the city fathers of Vegas would allow someone to be buried on commercial land a half-block off the strip.

"Can we go to Phyllis's office now?" Lucky says.

I follow his directions to PhySpa, then do a drive-by to check the lay of the land. I make a circle, pull into the parking lot, circle the building.

"Looks clear," I say.

Phyllis's car has been moved, so I park in her space and sit there a minute, looking around. It's too dark. Phyllis would want a light back here where her car is.

"Stay put," I say, then get out of the car and look around. By the time my eyes get to her roof line I notice her security light isn't working. I get back in the car, drive it to the business next door, and park behind their dumpster.

"I'm wearing heels, remember?" Gwen says.

"Why didn't you stay where you parked the first time?" Lucky says.

"The security light was aimed at us."

"So what? It was probably broken."

"It could be on a timer. If the timer's off by a few hours, the light could come on and attract attention."

"Wow," Gwen says. "You think of everything!"

"It was obvious," Lucky says. He's annoyed. I would be too, if I'd had a colonoscopy this morning and spent the last six hours on a plane.

Gwen picks up on it, too, and calls him sweetheart, as in, "Why are we here, sweetheart?"

"Creed and I have business here."

"What do you want me to do?"

"Come in with us, and sit tight."

"What are you gonna do?"

"Find something she hid."

"What?"

"I can't tell you. But it's important."

I park the car. As we remove our seatbelts, Lucky gets a call. I make eye contact with Gwen in the mirror. She blows me a silent kiss.

Lucky, on the phone, says: "Any way we can make it tomorrow? Well, does Surrey have to be there? Oh. Right. Well..." He looks at his watch. "Fifteen minutes? The Candlewood? Okay. Yeah, I'll get us a table. All right, we'll see you there."

"The Candlewood?" Gwen says, whining. "Really, Lucky? We'll be there all night!"

"Guy's got ten million to invest. He wants to eat at fuckin' Denny's, that's where we go."

"Can't it wait till tomorrow?" she says. "I'm tired."

"You believe this shit?" he says to me. "Twelve hours ago I'm in Jamaica with the Roto Rooter man adding a pipe extension up my ass, and this one's tired." He glances behind him. "You're always tired! When I was your age, I wanted to do it ten times a day. But you? You're too fuckin' tired. Tired from what? That's what I'd like to know."

"I'm sorry, Lucky," Gwen says. "I know you've had a bad day. Not to mention your fucking girlfriend got snuffed, and put my life in danger."

Lucky looks at me. "You believe this shit?"

"I'm not from here," I say. "What's the Candlewood, a restaurant?"

"Yeah," Lucky says. "A little off the beaten path. Good food, shitty service. But you won't notice either."

"Why's that?"

"Eddie's bringing Surrey with him."

"Who's that?" Gwen says.

"His wife."

"What, is she supposed to be beautiful or something?"

He laughs. "You'll see."

"How do I get there?" I ask.

"Go straight, get in the left lane. I'll tell you where to turn."

Ten minutes later, as we pull into the parking lot, Lucky says, "Gwen? Listen to me. Whatever happens, go with it."

"What's that supposed to mean?"

"You'll see. But don't fuck this up for me. I'm cash poor right now." To me, he says, "That doesn't apply to you. I've got your money, no sweat. I'll pay you in advance, when we get back to the house."

The parking lot is only half-full. I find a good spot, pull in, turn off the engine. Before we get out, Lucky puts his hand on my arm and says, "Prepare yourself."

"For what?"

"The strangest dinner meeting you'll ever attend."

17.

IF YOU WERE to ask, "Creed, what's the strangest dinner party you've ever attended?" I could tell you at least a half-dozen stories you'd be hard-pressed to believe. In my years overseas with the CIA I had numerous occasions to dine under extreme circumstances, during which I was often exposed to some of the zaniest, most bizarre situations imaginable.

In short, I don't know what you might consider the strangest. But to me, it's the time I saw tribesmen eating human feces at a dinner table in the jungle, sniffing it like a fine wine, touching it to note the texture, and savoring each mouthful as if it were the most delicate pâté de foie gras. It was all I could do not to gag, which probably would have caused an international incident, as fucked up as everyone gets in that part of the world over the most ridiculous things. After sampling from each pile and enthusiastically nodding, as though they could discern some subtle nuance of flavor between each morsel of turd, two warriors brought me a steaming pile of excrement no one else had been allowed to sample.

"No thanks," I said to the translator. "Sadly, I ruined my appetite eating bird shit all afternoon."

When he translated my message, the warriors grew agitated.

"You have just insulted the entire tribe," the translator

said. "And their wives."

"How did I manage to insult the wives?"

"Their wives worked all afternoon to create the meal. And the Chief's wife personally made your dinner."

I was about to ask what the hell he was talking about, then had that Oh, God! moment where I realized exactly what he was talking about. I tried not to picture the Chief's fat wife nude, squatting over the plank of wood they'd just brought me. But once an image like that is stuck in your head, it's there for the duration. I'm sure the look on my face had something to do with the sudden appearance of the Chief's knife at the dinner table.

The translator said, "The Chief's wife prepared your meal. It is the highest honor the tribe can bestow on an outsider."

I said, "See? This is why I hate my fucking job. It isn't enough we come in here and kill all their enemies, expand their safe zone, bring them medical supplies and save their godforsaken village. Now they're insulted, ready to kill me over a shit dinner."

With deep concern etched in his face, the translator said, "What should I say to the Chief?"

I sighed. "Tell him I apologize."

He did, then looked at me.

"Tell them I was unfamiliar with their customs."

He did, and they settled down a bit. One of them actually flashed me a shit-eating grin, an expression I haven't used from that day to this, and probably won't, ever again.

The tribesmen then passed me the turds anew, with great gusto, and stared at me with expectant eyes.

I picked up my walkie-talkie, pressed the button and waited for my unit commander to say, "Gray Fox Leader."

The tribesmen at the dinner table became agitated again,

and spoke to each other in frightened tones.

"Frank," I said.

"Sir?"

"I'm bringing you a doggy bag."

"I beg your pardon?"

"We're moving the dinner to your location. And you're going to eat it. With a big smile on your face. Or we're all going to die tonight. Do you understand?"

"Yes, sir."

"You and your second-in-command."

"Lieutenant Merriman?"

"That's right. Or someone wearing your uniforms, if you get my drift."

"Yes, sir. What about the rest of us?"

"Have your men set a line of explosives to include the lodge and as many huts as they can."

"To what effect, sir?"

"It's apparently very easy to offend these motherfuckers. If they so much as raise an eyebrow at us during dinner, we're taking them off the face of the planet tonight. These assholes don't need freedom. They need a fucking grocery store."

The Chief made a threatening gesture to the translator.

"What should I say to the Chief? He and his warriors are getting very upset."

"Tell him I can't accept an honor of this magnitude. Our customs dictate the recipient of such a gift be a representative of the American government. A man wearing a uniform with the symbol of our country on it."

I pointed to my shoulder. "I don't have a flag on my sleeve. But the representative does. We need to bring the dinner to our top leaders. The Chief has not yet met them."

The translator passed on the message, the meal was moved,

and Frank and Merriman's stand-ins got themselves a free dinner.

—So if you're asking, that was probably the most unusual dinner of my life.

Until tonight, in Las Vegas, when I meet Eddie Pickles and his wife, Surrey.

18.

WE'RE SEATED IN the center of the room at a table for five when "Fast" Eddie Pickles comes in and takes a seat next to me. After we're all introduced, he says, "A Jackson we see a cricket before a roach."

"You talking to me?" I say.

"He's offering you a bet," Lucky says. "Twenty dollars that we'll see a cricket before we see a roach. But you won't take that bet."

"Why not?"

"Because he's got a cricket in his pocket."

Eddie grins. "Didn't say it had to be a live cricket."

Lucky says, "A Franklin the bartender's got a Grant in his pocket."

Eddie says, "I'll take the under."

"Done."

The two of them head for the bar, leaving Gwen and me alone at the table.

"Is this a typical dinner for you?" I ask.

"Degenerate gamblers'll bet on anything," she says. "It's not about winning or losing. They crave the action."

"Who'll win this bet?"

"Can't say. The odds favor the under, but a bartender this time of night could easily be carrying more than fifty."

"Guess it pays to know the odds, huh?"

She laughs. "You wouldn't believe the odds these idiots can recite."

"Like what?"

"You want me to quiz you?"

"Go ahead."

"What are the odds of a woman dating a millionaire?"

"Ten thousand to one?"

"Two hundred fifteen to one."

"Really?"

"Yup. What are the odds a celebrity marriage will last a lifetime?"

"A hundred to one?"

"Three to one." She laughs. "You really suck at this."

I shrug. "Hit me again."

"Addicting, isn't it?"

"Give me another."

"What are the odds of being on a plane with a drunken pilot?"

"Five hundred to one."

She laughs.

"What?"

"You don't want to know."

"That bad?"

She nods.

"Tell me."

"One hundred seventeen to one."

"I may never fly again!"

"I tried to warn you."

"Try me again."

"Odds of an American speaking Cherokee?"

"A hundred thousand to one."

"Fifteen thousand to one."

"Are you making this up?"

"Nope. Odds of becoming President?"

"Three hundred million to one."

"Ten million to one. Odds of winning the California Lottery?"

"Five million to one."

"Thirteen million to one."

"Wait," I say. "Are you telling me I'm more likely to become President of the United States than I am to win the California Lottery?"

By way of answering she sings a sexy version of Happy Birthday that ends in "Happy birthday, Mr. President..."

"Marilyn Monroe?"

"Everyone knows that. But here's a good bet. Marilyn Monroe's dress size: under or over size 6."

"Under."

"Nope."

"She was a six?"

"Keep going."

"What? No way! She was a huge sex symbol."

"Huge is right. She was a size 12!"

"What? That doesn't make sense!"

"You're right. But you'd still lose your bet."

"Why?"

"Clothing sizes in the 1950s ran smaller. Marilyn's wardrobe proves she wore a size 12. But in today's dress sizes, she'd be a six. When you bet with these guys—and you shouldn't—you need to pay attention to each word. The bet was her dress size, not her actual size. Want to know something else strange about her?"

"Sure."

"She used to cut off one of her high heels to exaggerate her hip motion."

"I guess no one was looking at her feet," I say.

As the men come back, I hear Fast Eddie say, "So I check-raised the pigeon on the turn. When he come over the top with boys, I show pocket sharps!"

They roar. I look at Gwen. She shakes her head in disdain.

"Who won?" I say.

"Won what?" Eddie says.

"The bet just now."

"What bet?"

Lucky looks at Eddie and says, "Guy's got it bad, don't he!"

"Give me ten minutes with him," Eddie says, "I'll own his shorts."

He's on my left, Lucky's on my right, Gwen's sitting right of Lucky, which would put Surrey between Gwen and Eddie, if she were here.

After formally introducing me and Gwen to Fast Eddie, Lucky says, "Where's Surrey?"

"In the car," Eddie says. "Look, I want to apologize in advance for any tension we might bring to the dinner. But Surrey and I have been quarreling most of the day."

"About Vegas Moon?" Lucky says.

"No. About the pre-nup.

"It's a little late for that, isn't it?" Gwen says.

Lucky says, "They're not legally married yet."

Eddie adds, "It's all common law, so far." He smiles at Gwen. "But I intend to make an honest woman of her."

"Good for you!" Gwen says, enthusiastically. Then she looks at Lucky and adds, "That way, when you cheat on her, it'll raise your adrenalin."

"She understands!" Eddie says.

Gwen glances in my direction and says nothing, but her eyes are saying, Can you believe these assholes?

"Have you filed a legal action?" Lucky says.

"Not yet. We're still waiting and seeing. That's what lawyers like to do. Wait and see."

"But the meter keeps runnin', am I right?" Eddie says.

"Yeah. But hopefully those numbskulls in the state house will sign off on it."

Lucky said, "I know those guys. They tried to indict me for racketeering. Me, for Chrissakes! It's all I can do to keep the mob outta my business."

"Tell me about it," Eddie says.

"Is your last name really Pickles?" Gwen says. "Like in *Rugrats*?"

"What's *Rugrats*?"

"She's young," Lucky says. "Don't pay any attention to her."

"Hot as she is, it'd be impossible not to pay attention, if you don't mind my saying."

Gwen smiles, lowers her eyes, raises them again, working him. "Of course I don't mind, Eddie," she purrs.

Eddie smiles broadly. "I like it when you say my name like that," he says, while sexually assaulting Gwen's body with his eyes. "Jesus, Lucky! Now I know how you got the name! If I had something like that, I'd chain her to the bedpost and hit it day and night!"

Gwen notes my frown and shakes her head subtly, letting me know she's got this covered. She holds up her wrists and grins at Eddie. "See the handcuff marks? Thank God Lucky gave me a couple hours off tonight so I could meet you, 'cause he hammered it so hard my legs were like jelly."

Eddie is salivating. "You love it, don't you, baby! Oh yeah,

I can tell you love it."

Gwen smiles shyly. "Would you hate me if I told you I can't get enough?"

Eddie's jaw drops. Drops so hard his mouth remains open a minute. He just sits there staring at Gwen, with his mouth gaping open for so long I think he's forgotten to close it. Finally he turns to Lucky and gives him a look that's less like jealousy, more like envy. It's an evil look, just the same.

"Tell me the truth," he says. "How tight is she?"

Lucky smiles. "I probably shouldn't say."

Gwen says, "Thanks, Lucky."

Fast Eddie says, "C'mon. You gotta tell me. I gotta know."

Lucky says, "She's tighter than the skin on a grape."

"You lucky motherfucker!" he says.

"That's me," Lucky says, grinning. "And it'll be you, too, when you invest in Vegas Moon. I tell ya, Eddie, this is the real deal. We're gonna own Vegas, you an' me."

Eddie says, "I didn't love Surrey so much, I'd invite you and Gwen to a foursome."

Gwen looks like she's about to choke on bile. Which gives me time to wonder why Fast Eddie has to wait on a state court ruling to marry his girlfriend. Is she underage? Is she his cousin? I look at Eddie and decide it's probably his sister. But it wouldn't shock me to learn it's his daughter.

Lucky winks at Eddie and says, "You can't imagine what I might offer as a bonus to my biggest investors. In addition to cash dividends."

Eddie looks at Gwen, who somehow manages a faint smile. Then the words, "Who knows, indeed?" somehow escape her lips.

I wonder how many of these dinners she had to attend to help Lucky raise money for Vegas Moon, or other projects.

How many leers and rude comments has she already endured, or will be expected to endure in the future? How many times will she have to pretend to be impressed or "secretly" attracted to pigs like Eddie?

I look at this prick of a man to my left, and the one on my right who's possibly worse, and wonder how many bodyguards could work for assholes like these without becoming unraveled. I just met these guys and already want to kill them. But I'll continue doing my job, which is to sit quietly, scan the room, make sure no one hassles Mr. and Mrs. Peters. Since my life is on the line, I'll sit here and deal with it, long as I must, until I find the device.

The sound of a woman screaming near the door gets our collective attention.

"Surrey's here," Eddie says.

She is indeed.

She's actually being carried into the restaurant and over to our table by a guy Eddie introduces as Tom. Tom carefully places Surrey in her seat, and makes sure she's propped up.

Surrey's a doll.

Not a doll in the way you might say, "Oh, that Reece Witherspoon is so adorable! She's such a doll!"

No. Surrey's a life-sized, custom-made, one-hundred-pound, twenty-thousand-dollar doll, with skin and facial features so realistic, you have to do a double-take.

I look at the inanimate object sitting at the table. A few of her features are outsized, but in the best possible way. I'm not talking about her breasts, though now that I look, they appear outsized too.

Surrey's eyes are larger than her human counterparts', and her body type is petite with no hint of that emaciated look you get from super athletic women, or that hard, muscular look you see in women who lift weights every day. Surrey's lips are also enhanced, and her coloring appeals to me more than it probably should. Her ethnicity is enhanced, meaning she's multicultural, in a non-discernable way, as if some mad scientist created a perfect blend of female physicality from the world's most beautiful women. You look at Surrey and you see that technology and art have come together in perfect harmony, and all that's needed is a lightning strike to bring her to life.

Gwen's eyes are big as saucers.

"Surrey, what do you think about Vegas Moon?" Lucky says.

Eddie puts his ear to her mouth a minute, then says, "She just got her period."

"Excuse me?" Lucky says.

"I know," Eddie says. "Women, right? Jeez."

19.

I'VE READ ABOUT these dolls. They not only look real, they've been manufactured to feel real. Supposedly, their exterior is virtually identical to the texture of real flesh.

And speaking of flesh, the big draw for Fast Eddie Pickles and every other man who buys these dolls, is the sex. They have three entry areas, mouth, anal and vaginal. But unlike real women, when penetrated, these openings supposedly create a powerful suction. I'm not impressed. I bet a determined, properly motivated woman could give these dolls a run for their money.

Eddie puts his ear to Surrey's mouth again. Then says, "Surrey wants to apologize for being late. She's been crying, and didn't want her face to look puffy."

"Her face looks great!" Lucky says, which causes all of us to look at Eddie's doll. The realism is truly astonishing. Even her dead-eyed vacant stare and lack of general expression remind me of any number of women I've dated who would've preferred to be with someone else at the time.

Eddie leans over and puts his ear to Surrey's mouth, and then nods.

"What did she say?" Lucky says, shamelessly.

"She wants me to show you our pictures."

"What pictures?" Gwen says.

"We just got back from Costa Rica."

"No shit!" Lucky says.

"We had a great time, even though Surrey's parents refused to join us."

Gwen and I exchange a look, but Lucky keeps plowing ahead.

"Why not? Too busy? Passport problems?"

"They object to us living together out of wedlock. They're very strict."

Eddie reaches into his jacket pocket, pulls out a stack of five by seven prints. Hands them to me and says, "Pass 'em 'round."

There, depicted in full color, are photos of him and Surrey in Costa Rica. The first one shows Eddie and Surrey standing in front of a cab after arriving there. The second shows Eddie winking at the camera. I notice one of his hands is stuffed inside Surrey's shirt. Class act, this guy. In the background, the clearly rattled Costa Rican cab driver and Tom can be seen arguing. The third photo shows Eddie and Surrey trying to check into the hotel. The fourth shows Eddie attempting to bribe the police at the hotel. The fifth shows Surrey in a bikini, laying out by the pool. In the background, people are pointing and laughing. The sixth shows a crowd gathered around Surrey, and Tom working hard to keep them at bay. I skip through the stack, but have to stop when I come upon the shots of Eddie and Surrey at the zip line course. Surrey, in a crash helmet, being strapped into a harness. Her, flying through the air. Her, landing at the second platform, being "caught" by men with serious looks of concern on their faces. So severe are their facial expressions I can only assume Fast Eddie failed to let them know a life-sized doll was heading their way. They probably thought she'd suffered a heart attack.

I pass the photos to Lucky. He glances at them and makes what under normal circumstances would be appropriate comments, such as "Oh, I like this one!" and "Wow, nice outfit, Surrey!"

When he gets to the end, he passes them to Gwen, who bites her lip to keep from laughing. I dare not look at her for fear we'll both lose it.

Eddie leans over to Surrey again. Then speaks to me.

"Surrey thinks you're cute."

Gwen looks up from her stack of photos and smiles.

Lucky says, "The great thing about Vegas Moon is it's entirely sports-oriented. People can go there and bet the odds on any game being played that day, anywhere in the world. We'll have a hundred and fifty screens, all live action. Two thousand state-of-the-art reclining chairs, with betting machines built into the arms and a tray on the left for food and drinks. And a button they press to see a high-def virtual screen right in the middle of the air in front of them!"

While Lucky drones on, I feel Gwen's foot in my crotch. She's removed her boot somehow, and is rubbing me with her toes. I smile at her across the table. She smiles back. I put my hand on the top of her foot and lightly caress it with my fingertips. Her foot is cool to the touch.

Too cool.

I suddenly realize I'm playing with Surrey's foot.

I lift the tablecloth and see that Eddie has his left foot under Surrey's leg and is lifting and moving her foot against me. He sees me watching this take place, and suddenly jumps to his feet and yells, "What the fuck are you doing?"

He's yelling at Surrey, not me.

Gwen and Lucky look at me, as if I've done something wrong.

I shrug.

"You tramp!" Eddie yells. "You fucking whore!"

He slaps her hard across the face.

"Please," Lucky says. "I'm sure it was just a misunderstanding. It was just a misunderstanding, right, Surrey?"

Gwen looks at her husband and says, "Are you really this desperate?"

"That's it!" Eddie says. "I'm outta here!" He looks at Surrey. "Find your own way home, bitch!"

He stomps off, leaving Surrey with us at the table.

We're speechless.

As if proving Lucky right about the shitty service, a waiter appears for the first time since we were seated.

"Go fuck yourself!" Lucky says.

"Yes sir!" the waiter says with enthusiasm. He spins around and fairly sprints to the kitchen.

"You think he's going to?" Gwen says.

Lucky looks at me and says, "Well, I hope you're happy. Ten million dollars just walked out the door."

"You don't want to do business with that guy."

"Why not?

"Guys and Dolls? The media would have a field day."

Gwen laughs. "Pickles and Peters in business together. You get it? Pickled Peters?"

"Shut up, Gwen," Lucky says.

We all shut up. But our heads turn toward Surrey, as if caught in the pull of a tractor beam.

Moments later, Tom scurries over to the table. He appears to have tears in his eyes

"I'm so sorry!" he says, with great sincerity.

"Quite all right," Lucky says.

"I was talking to Surrey."

Gwen arches her eyebrow and says, "This gets weirder and weirder."

"I'll just escort her out of here," Tom says.

Gwen says, "He struck her!"

"He's upset," Tom says.

"I don't care! He can't just go around hitting her like that. It's still abuse."

Tom lowers his head and sighs.

"He's done worse."

He bites his bottom lip a moment, then positions himself behind Surrey, places his palms below her elbows, and carefully begins hoisting her to a standing position.

"This is the worst part," he says.

"Lifting her?" I say.

Tom shakes his head. "The constant fighting," he says. "They're always at each other's throats."

"Tom," I say.

"Sir?"

"What does he pay you?"

"Sir?"

"Eddie. How much does he pay you for this bullshit?"

"He doesn't pay me anything."

"Excuse me?"

"Surrey pays me."

Gwen laughs.

I say, "Of course she does."

20.

"IT'S NOT GOING to work, you know," I say to Lucky.

"What's not?"

"Your Vegas Moon scam."

"What are you talking about?"

"This isn't a real deal. And if it was, it wouldn't make sense."

"Why not?"

"You're the draw. The rest is just another sports book."

"What do you mean?"

"When you set the line at Vegas Moon, the casinos would simply adjust theirs. You'd be betting against yourself."

"You know anything about Vegas?"

"I know there's plenty of bank financing for legitimate deals."

We're in Phyllis's actual office. Gwen's walking through the other rooms with a penlight, keeping it below the windows the way I instructed her.

"You know much about sports betting?" Lucky says.

"Nope. But I understand people."

Gwen's light appears before she does.

"Where you been?" Lucky says.

"I wanted to see the lipstick message Phyllis left under the toilet seat."

"And?"

"It's not there."

"Cops must've took it as evidence."

She watches us work. Lucky's going through drawers. I'm pulling up part of the rubber baseboard.

"What were you boys talking about? I could hear you halfway across the office."

"Creed was telling me why he thinks Vegas Moon isn't going to work."

"Really? Why not?"

"Says he understands people. Doesn't know anything about Vegas or gambling, but he knows people."

"You probably get to know a lot about people when you watch them die," she says.

"You think I don't know people?" Lucky says. "I'm a professional gambler, for Chrissakes! Did you happen to hear the way I talked to Eddie a few minutes ago? How I changed my style and pattern of speech? I sell people what they want to buy, the way they want to buy it. Do you understand?"

"Yeah," she says. "You're a bullshit artist."

I'm smiling. Lucky can't see it, because the lights are aimed at our feet, but it's all over my face.

"I'm a pro, is what I am," Lucky says.

"You're a con artist," I say. "And desperation is coming off you like stink off a floater."

A half-hour passes as we continue looking for the device. Gwen's getting antsy, and I wonder if it's because she knows the device isn't here. I've studied her face since the moment we met, and I'm rapidly coming to the conclusion Phyllis lied about giving her the device. What would be her motive? Lucky's wife was her rival. Maybe she wanted me to torture, maim, or kill Gwen.

"We've got to get out of here," she says.

Lucky says, "Creed. You think the police found it?"

"No."

"Me neither. Let's see if we can break into her house."

"You got an address?"

"I can show you how to get there."

"You've been to her house?" Gwen says.

"I had to take papers there once," Lucky says.

"Lucky's quite the ladies' man," Gwen says.

"Used to be," he says. "Now I got you."

We sneak out the back of the office. As we make our way around the building, Lucky takes the lead. Gwen reaches behind her without looking and grabs my crotch. I reach around and grab her boob. Neither of us acknowledges the other, but she can tell I'm awake. As absurd as it is, we walk this way, hand-to-boob, hand-to-crotch, for a good twenty feet. Finally, I let go of her. She's still holding me tight, so I reach under her dress and slip my hand between her legs as she walks. She's surprised, and her voice catches in her throat. Comes out as a little squeal. We both remove our hands as Lucky says, "You okay?"

"Just caught my heel for a second," she says.

"Are you okay Mr. Creed?" she says, without turning around.

"Wait here," I say. "I'll get the car."

I'm in high school again. But having more fun this time around.

21.

"WHAT ARE YOU doing?" Lucky says.

"Pulling over."

"Something wrong?"

"You tell me."

I'd been heading toward Phyllis's house, but now I slow down to turn into the entrance of a Wendy's. I find an empty space and claim it. The sign light casts a yellow glow across part of the back seat where Gwen is sitting, and crosses her diagonally, illuminating her face, right arm and shoulder, leaving the rest of her in shadow. Lucky, in the front passenger seat, is directly in front of her. When he stares straight ahead like he's doing now, his face is backlit, and has an aura around it, that reminds me of a lunar eclipse. If the moon was wearing a cowboy hat.

Lucky's nervous, but acting cool. Gwen hasn't spoken since we entered the car. I see her giving me a quizzical look in the mirror. No one speaks for a minute.

Finally Gwen says, "Would you like to try a combo?"

"Shut up, Gwen," Lucky says. To me he says, "You know how late it is? I've been up twenty hours, nonstop. Not to mention my ass feels like the doctor left his scalpel in my upper intestine."

I say, "Lucky, look at me."

"Fine. I'm looking. What do you want?"

"I know what we're looking for. But I want to know what you plan to do with it."

He shrugs. "Phyllis had a device. A work product. I need it."

"Start at the beginning. But before you say anything, I'm going to allow you one lie."

"Excuse me?"

"You're going to tell me everything you know about the device, and how you first learned about it, and I'll let you lie up to one time. If I believe you're lying twice, I'll kill you without giving it a second thought. Do you believe me?"

"I don't know. You could be bluffing."

"Spoken like a gambler."

"Thanks."

"It's not a compliment."

I glance in the mirror and see the sudden flash of Gwen's smile as she realizes I just made a reference to what she said earlier in the day: that I was great-looking, but it wasn't a compliment. I give her a wink.

"Spill it," I say to Lucky. "I won't use this information against you. You have my word."

He pauses a few seconds, then says, "How much do you know?"

"I know a lot about the device. Things I haven't told you. But I need to know what you know, or we could be at a disadvantage with Connor Payne."

"What do you know about Ropic Industries?"

"I know you put twenty million bucks into a technology company that had a surplus of sixty million at the time. You bought your way onto the board, and worked a deal with your accountant to get your hands on twelve million of their investment capital. I think you took that money and bet it on college hoops, or pro football, or whatever the hell you like to bet on. And I think you lost your ass. So you went back to the trough for more money, and you lost that, too. I think you maxed out what you could get from the accountant, so you came up with this whole Vegas Moon bullshit. You can't get bank financing, so you're scamming your degenerate gambling friends, a million here, a half-million there. You're supposed to be using it to replace the money you stole from Ropic Industries, but you figure if you put it on the Lakers to beat Boston, you'll be able to repay twice as much. Only you're in a slump, and nothing's going your way. You know you'll dig out eventually, but you need some cash to get you through this slump. Meanwhile, you've got this device that Ropic manufactured, and somehow you're planning to cash in on it. Stop me if I'm wrong."

"You're wrong."

"Which part?"

"I don't want to do this in front of Gwen."

"She deserves to know what you've been up to."

"It's okay, Lucky," Gwen says. "You can tell the truth. I'll love you no matter what."

"You think?"

"I know. 'Cause you're a winner, Lucky. Everyone knows that."

He nods.

"Everything you said is true," Lucky says, "except the part about Vegas Moon, and the device."

"You've just told the first lie," I said. "Next lie kills you."

"It's not a lie! Not exactly."

Something in his voice makes me believe him. A little.

"Go on."

"Vegas Moon was my dream," he says. "I always planned

98

to build it. I put two million of my own money into it, and bought an option on the land. Then the bank crisis hit, and the regulators went ape-shit and forced the banks and insurance companies out of the project. So I tried to raise the money myself. But the economy is so fucked up, only a few people invested. It wasn't enough to start the project. So I used Ropic's money as a nest egg for my bets. I figured if I could win enough, I could pay Ropic back, with interest, and break ground on Vegas Moon. Here in Vegas, once you break ground, the money starts pouring in."

I think about what he says, and decide it could have gone down that way.

"Okay, you can have your lie back. Now tell me about the device."

"I liked Ropic because, like you said, they had a lot of cash, and no one knows this, but the accountant was one of my employees. He'd made money with me before, but never had any real cash to bet. Plus, he was frustrated, tired of counting other people's money all day. I convinced him I had some locks, some sure-thing bets, and kicked him back fifty grand for every million he got me. He used his share to mirror my bets, meaning, we both lost everything. But there was another reason I liked Ropic: their research team owned patents on super-secret technology the government needed for high-tech weapons. For a corporation that size, a government contract would have made the stockholders rich."

"But that didn't work out."

"Right. Because the new administration cut the funding, and the military backed out. Our products had no use beyond weaponry that's illegal for civilians to own. I thought about selling it to the enemy, but our tech people said no one else has the technology. Our devices were just one piece of a sophisticated weapons system. So I called a board meeting and said, 'What the fuck do we own that we can make money with?' And the answer was 'Nothing.' Can you believe it? Ropic had all their eggs in one government basket.

"So the board says, 'Good thing we've got that sixty million dollars. We can buy some technology, stamp our name on it, and start a whole new dog and pony show.' And that's when me and Stevie went into a panic."

"Stevie the accountant?"

"Right."

"I'm falling asleep here, Lucky. Tell me about the device."

"After the board meeting, Phyllis—Dr. Willis, I mean, brought me a little metal box. It was like something you'd see in the movies. She said, 'What I'm about to tell you, no one knows.' She said she went to a secret government facility and watched a doctor implant a heat chip into Connor Payne's brain. The chip has a four-digit code that can be entered from anywhere in the world by using a remote unit that looks like a large wristwatch. When you punch a code into the wrist unit, the chip will instantly kill Mr. Payne."

"Jesus!" Gwen says.

"Right. And then Dr. Willis said that the government thought they had the only two wrist devices ever made, but Ropic Industries actually had three more that no one knew about."

"Three?"

"Three."

"Are you sure about that?"

"That's what she said. Five wrist devices were manufactured."

Darwin had one, Doc Howard had the second, which he sold to me for a hundred million bucks. I took Phyllis's unit with me after killing her. Which leaves two wrist devices unaccounted for.

"Where are they?" I ask.

"Phyllis had one. I don't know what happened to it. Probably the cops have it. But this morning—or is it yesterday morning?—anyway, Connor Payne showed up at Phyllis's office. She figured he knew about the device and planned to kill her. So she input the code, thinking he'd die in her lobby. But it didn't work."

"And why's that, do you suppose?"

"Someone must've reprogrammed the chip."

"But there's a small device in a metal box that Phyllis gave you."

"Right. That little device can override any code. You plug it into one of the wrist units, punch in any four numbers, and the chip will boil Mr. Payne's brains anywhere in the world."

"Were you planning to blackmail Mr. Payne?"

"Hell no! You think I'm crazy? The whole thing gave me the creeps. I told Phyllis I didn't want any part of it. Told her to hide the device and never tell me where she put it. But Connor Payne has to know about the device."

"If he doesn't have it, he might start killing Ropic board members until he finds it?"

"Exactly," Lucky says.

"So you hope to find the chip, place it with a wrist unit, and kill Conner Payne?"

"Yes. In self-defense."

"A pre-emptive strike."

"Exactly."

"Only now you can't find the wrist unit or the device."

"Right. But if I get the chip back, maybe I can find out who has the other wrist units."

It was giving me a sick feeling too, wondering who might have them.

"You should have a record of the sales," I say.

"I doubt they were sold. I don't know what happened to them. Maybe they're locked away in a storage container somewhere."

I think about it from Lucky's point of view. "This whole Connor Payne thing has sidetracked you from raising money to recover your losses."

"It has."

"As I see it, you need two things: Connor Payne out of your life, and capital to finance your play till your luck changes."

"Exactly."

"Let's go home, get some rest. I'll keep Connor Payne at bay while you meet more investors."

"I still want to search Phyllis's house. I doubt we'll find anything, but we need to try."

"It's your call," I say.

He thinks about it a minute. "Let's look for an hour. If we don't find it, we'll just have to live in fear."

In the back seat, Gwen groans.

"What?" Lucky says.

"I'm starving."

To me he says, "Can you go through the drive-through, get her some fries or something?"

I give him a look.

"Please, Mr. Creed?" Gwen says. "I love french fries."

I look at her in the mirror. She licks her lips in a way that indicates far more than her love of french fries.

To Lucky I say, "You want anything?"

"Diet Coke."

"And a shake," Gwen says. "If you don't mind."

"Uh huh." Long as I'm a waiter, might as well go all in. "Anything else, Mr. Peters?"

"No," Lucky says, "just the drink. And get yourself something. I'm buying."

Something in his tone. Disrespect? Or maybe I just don't like the man. I think about how he made his housekeeper, Tina, work tonight, and feel a twitch, the kind I get when bad things start to go down.

Lucky's staring straight ahead, his eyes focused on something outside the car. Probably calculating the odds on what color car might turn into the lot next. His hands are in his lap, and all I can think of is how careless he is to offer me complete access to two unguarded targets. I'm three feet away. I could kill him two different ways with a single strike. He's left me not only the temple, but the jugular as well. Temple or jugular. Temple or…"

"Mr. Creed?" Gwen says. "Fries?"

I glance in the mirror.

She does that tongue thing again, and now I'm thinking fries.

That's me, in the white rental car. Donovan Creed, deadliest man on earth. Ordering fries, a Diet Coke, and a shake at the Wendy's drive-through. Telling the guy, "I'm only going through this line once, son. Don't fuck up my order." Him saying, "Relax, Pops. I'm on it."

Pops?

22.

I DRIVE PAST Phyllis's house, turn the corner, and park the car. I tell them to wait two minutes, then circle the block, and drive the car right into the garage.

"You can break in that fast?" Gwen asks.

"Faster. But I want to check the house before you guys enter, to make sure it's safe."

"Why wouldn't it be?" Lucky says.

"Connor Payne."

"Good point."

I have zero interest in searching Phyllis's house for the second time in thirty hours. Gwen doesn't want to be here either. She's tired and bored, and it wouldn't take much to set her off. Lucky's a different beast. He claims to be exhausted, but gamblers have legendary stamina. They can sit at a poker table for three, four days at a time and never lose the ability to concentrate. In other words, fatigue is not going to make him quit. On the bright side, he's losing faith in the device, because even if he finds it, he won't be able to use it without the wrist unit.

I'm not the type of guy to purposely create friction in a marriage unless I'm trying to kill the husband or bang the wife. And even though I'd love to bang Gwen, it doesn't appear I need to do much more than show up with a bag of fries to make that happen. But since I'm ready to call it a day,

I decide to manipulate them into a major argument.

I break into Phyllis's house quickly, and make my way to her bedroom. From my jacket pocket I retrieve the gift-wrapped box, the one that contains Lucky's cufflinks and a condom, and the note that says, "Your turn to get lucky!" I place the box on top of the nightstand next to her bed. As I head down the hall I can practically hear the time bomb ticking. Then I go to the garage and press the button to open the door.

23.

IT'S A LONG ride back to Lucky's house. The two are barely speaking to each other.

When they entered Phyllis's house a few minutes ago, I arranged it so Lucky and I would start searching Phyllis's office, and Gwen could check the bedroom. It took about ten seconds for her to notice the gift, and she brought it to us immediately.

"Should I open it?" she said.

I asked Lucky, "Does it look about the right size?"

He nodded.

"Go ahead," I said.

She did.

She didn't get mad.

She exploded with fury.

"You motherfucker!" she yelled. Then threw the box at him and stormed out of the house and sat in the car.

"She'll warm up by the time we get home," he said.

"You think?"

We gave up the search and went to the car. Lucky apologized to Gwen for what she'd seen, but claimed the gift didn't prove they'd ever had sex. According to him, it meant she wanted to have sex with him. Gwen clung to a more literal translation.

"The note said, 'Your turn to get lucky.'"

"So?"

"It didn't say, 'Do you want to get lucky?'"

"I don't get your point," Lucky said.

"The point is, go fuck yourself."

Twenty minutes later I'm pulling into their driveway. The gate goons wave us through, and I park in the same place I parked earlier in the day. Gwen gets out of the car first and stomps toward the front door, while fishing her keys out of her purse. Lucky's rushing to catch up. I get his bags out of the trunk and follow them inside. Gwen starts making a beeline to their bedroom. Lucky notices me and says, "Where do you think you're going?"

Gwen stops abruptly and turns around.

"I was planning to check the house."

"And then?"

"Stay in the room Tina set up for me."

"No way."

Gwen and I exchange a glance. She says, "You hired him to protect us, asshole."

"He can protect us from outside."

"What's the problem?" I say.

"You want to know the problem?"

I shrug. "It's why I asked the question."

"The problem is, forty-five minutes ago you threatened to kill me. And now you think I'm going to let you sleep in my home?"

"If you don't need me here, pay me what you owe and I'll head back to LA."

"You signed on for a week. For the next seven nights, you can sleep in your car."

"Pay me now and I will."

"I don't keep that much cash at the house. I'll pay you tomorrow."

"Then tomorrow night I'll sleep in the car."

He starts to say something, then sees Gwen moving quickly toward the bedroom. He runs to catch up. She gets there first and tries to slam the door. Lucky wedges his foot in the threshold just in time to keep from getting locked out, but the blow to his foot makes him cry out in pain.

There's a lot of yelling between them and I catch myself chuckling at some of the combinations of curse words Gwen strings together. I know she doesn't want me to see her act this way, but she can't help herself. And Lucky isn't helping his cause by yelling back.

"I hate to interrupt," I say. "But I should check out that wing of the house."

"I'll take my chances," Lucky says. "I don't want you in the command center."

"You can check out the bedroom and closet," Gwen says.

As I enter the bedroom, Lucky rushes over to the door that leads to his command center and blocks it.

"I don't care what you do in there," I say. "I'm just trying to keep you safe."

"If Connor Payne has been in there, I may as well be dead anyway. He can do what he wants to me."

"I hope he does," Gwen says. "I can't believe you did that to me. Turned my name into a scam."

"What name?" I say.

"Vegas Moon," Gwen says.

"You came up with it?"

She starts to answer, but Lucky says, "Shut up, Gwen."

And she does.

The bedroom is large, but there's no place for anyone to hide except behind the curtains or under the bed. I check the curtains first. Then, feeling like an idiot, I get on my hands and knees and check under the bed, thinking it would serve me right if Connor Payne was under there. I check the windows, and the door that leads to the patio.

"Everything's fine," I say.

"Please check the closet," Gwen says.

"Oh, yes, please do!" Lucky says, his voice dripping with sarcasm.

Their closet is enormous. At least six hundred square feet.

I walk through it as slowly as possible, trying to decide where Gwen might have hid the device. We're talking about a white piece of ceramic that's smaller than a dime. I notice twelve custom drawers on her side, six on his. There are numerous rows of shoes and boots and several racks of clothes. Lou Kelly told me Lucky and Gwen got married five months ago after a very brief courtship. That being the case, I'm amazed how many clothes she's managed to accumulate this quickly. I move my hands through her dresses, pretending to check that no one's hiding behind them.

As I exit the closet, Lucky says, "Don't stay up late. We've got a breakfast meeting at eight."

"I'm not going," Gwen says.

Lucky says, "You might wish you had, if Connor Payne shows up."

"He can't be much worse than you," she says.

Lucky looks at me. "It's such a joy to be home," he says. "You can't imagine."

Gwen looks at him and says, "If your ass still hurts, I'll be glad to pound some ice up your rectum."

24.

GWEN DECIDES TO go with us to breakfast after all, which tells me Lucky convinced her how badly they need the cash. Lucky's mark is Hampton Hill, who insists on meeting us at Hometown Hearth. When he orders ham and hash Gwen and I exchange a look.

"Everything is double H's with this guy," Lucky says, by way of explanation. Then, filling his voice with warmth, he adds, "While I've only known Hampton a short time, he's already one of my dearest friends. He says the double H has always brought him luck."

"H's are like undertakers," Hampton says.

"How's that?" I say.

"They're the last ones to let you down."

Gwen, bless her heart, pretends to giggle, which brings a broad smile to Hampton's face.

"You're so cute!" she squeals. "I can see why Lucky adores you so!"

"Well, aren't you just the sweetest little thing!" he says.

"Why, thank you, Hampton!"

He looks at Lucky and says, "Fifty the waitress is married."

Lucky says, "No way. You eat here all the time."

"Then you pick the bet."

Lucky says, "Fifty her youngest kid was born after June 30th."

"Bullshit bet. There's three less days in the first half of the year."

This goes back and forth until they finally agree on a bet. Hampton calls the waitress over. She says, "Your food's not ready yet, hon."

Lucky says, "Think of a number between one and a hundred."

She smiles. "You boys bettin'?"

"We might be."

"Seventy-three," she says.

Hampton claps his hands. "Pay up!"

Lucky frowns. "How'd you come up with that number?"

"Just entered my brain," she says. Then winks at Hampton.

"Son of a bitch," Lucky says, forking over the cash. "How many things does she have to remember for you?"

"'Bout a hundred."

Gwen smiles and says, "That's smart planning."

Hampton gives her a long look, licks his lips and says, "I bet kissin' you is like lickin' sugar off a baby's arm."

Gwen looks gobsmacked, but recovers quickly. She winks at him and says, "I wonder if you'll ever get the chance to find out about my kisses."

"I'd pay good money to find out right now!" he says, grinning like Death eating a cracker.

Hampton has wretched teeth and long, stringy hair and reminds me of the pervert we used to see sniffing bicycle seats at our junior high school.

I notice Lucky's content to sit back and let Gwen charm the mark.

"What do you do for a living, Hampton?" Gwen asks.

"I own a research company. We do product testin'."

"That sounds fascinating! What are you working on right now?"

"You ever see those moist tissue wipes in the toilet paper aisle?"

Gwen says, "We use those! Don't we, Lucky?"

"We do for a fact."

"Did you test those?"

Hampton says, "Depends on the brand you're usin'. We tested Beau Fresh. Thanks to my company, Beau Fresh can advertise 'Thirty-eight percent cleaner than regular toilet paper'."

Gwen says, "Someone actually tests that sort of thing?"

"It's very scientific," Hampton says. Then he looks around the room and lowers his voice. "But I'll let you in on a little secret, if you promise not to tell."

Gwen doesn't know what to say, so she just sits there with a fake smile frozen on her face.

Hampton says, "They paid me to test a hundred samples from a hundred people over a thirty-day period. But me and four employees did all the shittin' in one day! You got any idea how much profit that is?"

Gwen's reeling. She needs a lifeline. Lucky throws her one.

"Hampton's a helluva businessman, isn't he!"

"It's a truly remarkable story," Gwen agrees.

Lucky and Gwen work well together. By nine a.m., Hampton's trying to talk Lucky into giving him a hundred-thousand-dollar share for eighty-eight grand.

"H is the eighth letter of the alphabet," Hampton says. "Eighty-eight thousand would be a double H."

Lucky's ready for him. "If you write out a check for $88,000.00, that's only seven digits. $100,000.00 is eight digits."

Hampton counts it out and frowns.

"You can do it," Gwen urges.

He looks at her. "I'll kick in the extra twelve if you let me squeeze them titties one time."

Gwen looks at Lucky with trepidation.

Lucky pauses a moment, then says…"Be gentle."

The effect those two words have on Gwen is almost more than I can bear. The spark of magic I'd seen in her eyes quickly drains away, along with whatever youthful innocence she may have clung to before he uttered them. In the space of two words, Lucky Peters killed something inside his wife, something I believe was special and sacred. I hate him for doing it, and for making me watch.

Hampton writes the check and hands it to Lucky. Then starts reaching his hands toward Gwen's boobs. She closes her eyes, bites the corner of her lower lip, trying not to cringe.

But Hampton doesn't get titty at this time.

In fact, he's already forgotten about Gwen's boobs because I've got him by the throat. I lift him from his chair and drag him out the door and shove him into my car. He's trying to talk, but nothing comes out until I release my grip on his windpipe. But now all that's coming out is a raspy sound. While he's trying to speak, I remove his wallet and read his address out loud, memorizing it. I glance in the window of the restaurant and see Lucky and Gwen trying to calm down the cashier. I watch a minute, to make sure she's not calling the cops. Then say, "Do you have a wooden banister at home?"

"Wh-what?"

"A wooden banister. A railing."

"Y-yes. On the st-steps."

"Hampton, look at me." When he does, I say, "Do yourself a favor, okay?"

He nods.

"Cooperate."

"I w-will."

"I know you're going to feel a lot braver after I let you go. I won't seem so scary an hour from now, and it's human nature for you to want to lash out at someone. You'll probably go to the cops."

"N-no. N-never."

I take a rag from the glove compartment and tie it around his head to make a blindfold.

"If you do decide to call the cops, I'll hunt you down and nail your nuts to the banister. Wait. You probably don't believe me."

"I d-do."

"No you don't. Because people say things like that all the time, but they don't mean them. The funny thing is, you're going to assume I'm like everyone else. And when I leave you standing on tiptoes with your hands tied behind your back and your nuts nailed to the banister you're going to think about how you should've believed me. Within minutes your knees are going to start shaking. When you try to stand flat-footed, you'll find the only way to accomplish that is to tear your ball sack. You'll put it off as long as possible, which in my experience is two hours, max. Eventually you'll do what they all do."

"Wh-what?"

I decide not to tell him. Letting him imagine the worst is more terrifying.

Lucky and Gwen come out of the restaurant. Lucky's furious. He marches up to the driver's window, starts banging on it, demanding me to open up. Gwen passes in front of the car, staring directly at me, mouthing the words, Thank you!

It might be wishful thinking, but I think I see the spark returning to her eyes. I give her a wink, then roll the window down an inch and say, "Back up, Lucky. I'm getting out."

To Hampton I say, "Sit tight."

"Can I take off my blindfold?" he whines.

"No."

I turn the radio on so he won't hear the quick conversation I have with Lucky and Gwen. Then I climb back in the car, turn the radio off, and say, "Lucky is very angry at me. He's a man of his word, and Gwen's a good sport. Against my wishes, she's agreed to let you feel her up."

"It's okay. I w-was out of line."

Lucky opens the door. Gwen is standing next to him. She reaches out and takes his right hand in hers.

"I want you to," she coos. "Please?"

"Okay."

Lucky lifts up his shirt, exposing the sensational pair of breasts Gwen showed me in the photo. It only takes a quick glance to confirm that Phyllis put a lot of love into his boob job. Good thing, because one glance is all I can stomach. To me, it's just creepy. Gwen places Hampton's hand on Lucky's left tit. His hand jumps. He obviously wasn't expecting to touch flesh. He touches it again, enthusiastically, and Gwen moans softly. This goes on long enough that I have to bite my tongue to keep from laughing. Finally, Gwen removes Hampton's hand from Lucky's breast, leans into the car and gives Hampton a kiss on the cheek. Whispers something in his ear. I motion Lucky and Gwen to get in the back seat. They do, and I drive us to Hampton's bank to cash the check. When we get there, Lucky and Gwen take the check inside. When they exit the bank moments later, they're not happy.

"What's wrong?"

"Insufficient funds."

"How much does he have?"

"They won't say."

I remove his blindfold.

"How much is in your account?" I say.

"A couple hundred."

"Dollars?" Lucky says. "You son of a bitch!"

I kick Hampton out of the car. As we drive away, he yells, "Gwen! Call me!"

A few minutes later Gwen says to Lucky, "Now you know what it's like."

"What?"

"To get felt up by a slime ball."

"Actually, I kind of liked it," Lucky says.

25.

WE'RE BACK AT the house. Gwen's in her bedroom, changing clothes. Lucky's in his command center, with the door locked. He's settling back into his routine. After missing several days of action, the calls from his savants are piling up. I'm on the phone with Callie, telling her about my morning. When I hear Gwen open her bedroom door, I say, "Gotta run!" and click my phone off.

"Will you take me to the Forum?"

She's wearing cut-off jeans with frayed ends that are short enough to show a sliver of pink panty, and a UNLV cotton T-shirt with rhinestone lettering. A thin, tan leather strap hangs on one shoulder and crosses her chest like a bandolier belt, and is attached to a Chanel purse that hugs her left hip. The purse is high style, but too small to be practical. She's wearing pink eyeshadow, with blue eyeliner, and frosted pink lipstick. Her hair's in a pony tail and the whole package is put together so well, I don't give a shit what kind of sandals she's wearing. But they look great, too.

"The shopping center Forum?" I say.

"The same."

"What about Lucky?"

"He won't even know we're gone."

"You sure about that?"

"Trust me. He'll stay locked in there till eight-fifteen tonight."

"Why?"

"Two reasons. First, he's avoiding you."

"Why?"

"He's afraid you're going to ask for your money."

"And?"

"He doesn't have it."

I shrug. "No big deal."

"No?"

"I don't need the money."

We walk out the back door, lock it behind us, and get in my car.

After settling into the passenger seat, Gwen looks at me with curiosity. "If you don't need the money, why'd you take the job?"

"Honestly? I wanted to get to know you."

I glance at Gwen's face while I start the car. She looks surprised. I drive us down the driveway, wave at the gate goons, and turn right. It's hot out, and in the distance I can see wavy heat lines coming off the asphalt.

The lots are nice in this area, with oversized houses, and massive iron gates designed to make honest people feel safe.

But they're not safe.

Each of these homes is a cracker box to guys like me.

"Why were you interested in knowing me?" Gwen says.

"Specifically, I wanted to determine if you were the type of woman who could look me in the face and lie, even when the truth would serve you better."

She laughs. "And what have you decided?"

"You are."

She scrunches her nose. "Well, that's not very flattering."

"Do you deny it?"

She leans over and kisses me on the cheek. "No. But let me say this: I only lie to level the playing field."

"That's well put," I say. Then ask, "What's the second reason?"

"For what?"

"Back at the house you said there were two reasons why Lucky would stay locked up in his command center till eight-fifteen. The first is he's avoiding me. What's the second reason?"

She turns away and looks out the window.

I try again: "What happens at eight-fifteen?"

"That's when he comes out for his shower."

"And why's there a timetable for that?"

"Because Maddie's coming."

"Wait. Tonight?"

"At nine."

"Maddie, as in threesome Maddie?"

"It's not a threesome. Lucky doesn't participate."

"No?"

"He watches."

We come to the first light just as it turns red. It turns out to be a long light, considering how little traffic there is out here.

I look at her and say, "Do you enjoy being with Maddie?"

She scrunches her nose again. "It's not really my thing. I mean, I'm a willing participant. If I'm in the mood."

"Really?"

"You're giving me that old guy look again," she says.

"Oh. Sorry. I don't mean to."

"What then?"

"The thing you said about being with Maddie."

"What about it?"

"I like it. I think. I'm just trying to understand."

"Maddie's one of a kind. Teeny Tiny, but a sexual rock star. So when she comes over, it's like an event. Between the X, the booze, the music, and the sheer force of Maddie's sexuality, I can get caught up in it."

"If you're in the mood."

"That's right."

The light finally turns green. I drive to Capstan Way, take a left, and follow it all the way to the interstate.

"And if you're not in the mood?"

Gwen laughs. "Maddie doesn't need me to participate. She just prefers that I do."

"Maybe I should be there tonight, just in case."

She giggles. "In case Maddie tries to kill us?"

"No. In case you're in the mood."

She smiles. "I won't be."

"No?"

She whispers, "Not if things go according to plan."

I whisper back, "What's the plan?"

She whispers, "I'll tell you in the hotel room."

"What hotel room?"

She laughs again. "You stopped whispering."

"I got excited. What hotel room?"

"You didn't really think I wanted you to take me shopping, did you?"

In truth, that's exactly what I thought. I mean, I've seen her closet.

She says, "I was thinking you could drop me off at the mall entrance, park the car, and get us a room at Caesar's."

"And then?"

"I'd meet you there."

"That's what you thought?"

"Unless you're chicken."

26.

GWEN CALLS FROM the lobby. I give her the room number, then say, "I'll leave the door slightly open so you can walk in without knocking."

"That's very thoughtful of you," she says.

Moments later she enters the room, turns her back to me while closing the door, and locks the dead bolt. In the movies, this is where she spins around, holding a gun on me. The audience gasps in shock! But of course this ain't the movies, and Gwen doesn't have a gun. Her purse is too small, remember?

She crosses the floor, puts her arms around my waist, holds me tight. Then she tilts her chin and kisses me with good intentions. I kiss her back with bad ones. We go at it awhile, good and bad intentions, moving around the room, backing into the desk, her against the wall, me against the wall, neither of us against the wall, all the while making breathless moaning sounds. We sound silly, like teenagers imitating movie romance.

But laughing is not an option.

Success in fighting means not coming at your opponent the way he wants to fight you. Success in lovemaking is just the opposite: you've got to come at her the way she wants to fuck you. And tomorrow she'll want you to come at her a different way. I'd give you the whole seminar, but I'm too busy right now. Plus, she's asking me something.

"You've wanted to do this since the day we met," she says.

"Yes."

I decide not to remind her we met exactly twenty-eight hours ago.

She breaks the embrace and backs up to the bed, removes her sandals, and sits down. A small cloud passes over her face.

"What's wrong?"

"I want to say something," she says. "About this morning."

I kick off my shoes and sit beside her on the bed. She scoots to the far side and lies down, motions me to join her. When we're face to face, she gives me a small kiss. I trace my fingertips over her thigh, from the end of her shorts to her knee, and back again.

"What about this morning?" I say.

"I wanted to thank you for what you did."

"At the restaurant?"

"Uh huh."

I lean over and kiss her, softly.

"My pleasure," I say.

She raises up to a sitting position and reaches her hands behind her head to unroll the scrunchie from her ponytail. Then tosses her head a single time, and ah, the joys of youth: every hair falls magically into place. Except for one tiny wisp that's hanging over her eye. I reach up and smooth it to the side.

We kiss again, a quick peck, and she says, "You haven't asked why Lucky would allow that man to feel me up at the restaurant."

"No."

"How come?"

"I try not to judge people."

"You just execute them?"

"I'd like to dress it up nicer than that," I say, "but…"

"It is what it is?"

"It is."

We kiss again.

"Can I ask you a question?" she says.

"Of course."

"Promise you won't try to read too much into it?"

"I'll try."

"How much would you charge to kill Lucky?"

27.

"UNDER NORMAL CIRCUMSTANCES what would I charge to kill your husband? Or are you asking what I would charge you?"

"Both."

"Under normal circumstances, that's a hundred-thousand-dollar hit."

"And for me?"

"Is that what we're doing here today? Making a contract?"

She gives me three short, quick kisses.

"God, I love your face!" she says.

I wait for her to answer my question. She finally says, "I don't want you to kill Lucky."

"No?"

"Of course not."

"Then why'd you ask?"

"I'm trying to understand you."

That surprises me. "In what way?"

"I'm trying to understand how you place a monetary value on other people's lives."

The woman lying on the bed with me today is far shrewder than the girl I met yesterday. Today's woman is probably smarter than me, which is a plus, if we're in a relationship. But right now we're on a bed in a hotel room, and there's fire in my pants. I want yesterday's girl to put it out. I sigh, realizing today's woman is waiting for me to answer her question about how I price my hits.

"There are a lot of factors that go into the equation," I say.

"Such as?"

"His prominence, how hard it would be to kill him, if there was a specific time and place you needed it done, and if you require a specific method."

"Of killing him?"

"Yes."

"So it could cost more."

"Or less."

"Interesting."

"How much to kill Carmine?"

"Excuse me?"

"Carmine Porrello, crime boss, western region."

"I know who he is."

"Would you take a contract that big?"

I shrug. "It's what I do."

"You could kill Carmine?"

She's looking at me with bright, hopeful eyes.

I meet her gaze. When I speak, my words are clear and precise.

"I can kill anyone."

The smile that spreads across her face says she likes my answer.

I say, "Anything else you want to ask?"

"Yes. Are you ever going to fuck me?"

28.

WE FUCKED.

It wasn't love, but it wasn't bad. Not even close to the best sex either of us has had, but probably the best sex either of us is likely to have today. Unless Gwen decides she's in the mood tonight when Maddie shows up.

After our breathing gets back to normal, Gwen moves in close to cuddle me. I hadn't thought about it till now, but I realize we're still on top of the covers.

"I hope we can do it again in a few minutes," she says, touching me down there, as if trying to determine how many minutes it might be.

"I'd like that," I say, trying to avoid thinking I might be on a timetable.

"You're the best I ever had," she says.

"Really?"

"Swear to God."

"You, too," I say. Then add, "Speaking of lies, there's something I haven't told you or Lucky. About Phyllis."

She sits up. I'd love to describe for you how the sheet falls away slowly, revealing her perfect, artificially enhanced breasts, but I already told you we're on top of the covers.

Not that it makes her boobs any less attractive.

"What haven't you told us?" she says, her voice suddenly serious.

"If I tell you a big secret, will you tell me one?"

"Like truth or dare?"

"Except without the dare."

"Okay. Wait. Who gets to choose the subject?"

"Me."

"That might be fun," she says. Then adds, "Do I have to tell the truth?"

"That's sort of the whole purpose."

She frowns. "Well, I can try, right? So what's your big secret about Phyllis?"

"I met her."

She's quite surprised. "When?"

"Yesterday."

"Before Connor Payne killed her?"

"Yes. And I asked her about the device."

"The one we've been looking for?"

I nod.

"How did you know about it?"

"Connor's been seeking it awhile."

"He spoke to you about it?"

"We're getting off track. Let's just say I was trying to negotiate a deal with Phyllis, to keep Connor from killing her."

"She paid you off?"

"No. I was just seeking the device."

"And she didn't give it to you?"

"No."

"Why not?"

"She didn't have it."

She stares at me. "Who does?"

"According to Phyllis, you."

"What? Me?"

"She told me she gave it to you."

"For what purpose?"

"To hide?"

"I hardly even knew the bitch! And she hated me, remember?"

"I've got your word for that."

Gwen frowns. "I see. And we've already established I'm a liar."

"Just to level the playing field," I say.

She gives me a look that's not quite anger, but awfully close. "You're totally killing the mood here, you know."

"I know."

Gwen's on the verge of throwing a pout. I'm okay with that. I'm trying to accomplish two things here. First, I want to know if she's got the device. Second, I want to get laid again, and see if we can improve the experience by coming at her a different way. On the one hand, I don't want to make her too angry. On the other, I need to secure the device.

I say, "If it makes you feel any better, I believe you."

She turns both palms up. "You'd have to. Phyllis was fucking my husband. We didn't like each other. She wouldn't have given me anything important, and I wouldn't have accepted it if she had."

"At the time she told me, it made sense. Now that I understand the relationship, it doesn't. Are you sure she hated you?"

"Yes. And Lucky didn't make things any easier by rubbing her nose in it."

"What do you mean?"

"He made her give me all those spa treatments, plastic surgery, chemical peels..."

"She didn't charge him?"

"Well, of course she did."

"Well, isn't that why she's in business?"

"Do you know anything about women?"

I take a breath before answering.

"No. I talk a good game…but no. Every time I think I've finally got a handle on women, I realize the handle isn't connected to anything. In the end, I'm just holding a handle, without a clue."

"It was a rhetorical question."

"Oh."

"God, you're good-looking when you do that," she says.

"Do what?"

"That whole clueless thing. You need to cultivate it. It works for you."

This is something I already know. And she's right. It does work. Problem is, it's not an act.

"Let me give it to you from a woman's perspective," she says.

"Okay."

"I'm young and sexy, Phyllis is a drone. I'm not being cocky or putting her down. These are the facts. Phyllis wanted Lucky. Don't ask me why, but let's assume she wanted him."

"Okay."

"They probably met around the time Lucky and I got married. They were certainly having sex before Lucky made her start fixing my flaws."

"You're saying she didn't like the idea of making you even more appealing to him?"

"Exactly."

"Because she considered you her rival?"

"There may be hope for you yet."

I think about that a moment, and then it hits me.

I know exactly where the device is hidden.

Gwen touches the area between my legs and says, "I think we're getting close here."

"I agree."

"I bet if I lick your lollipop I can make you big and strong. Would you like that?"

Would I like that?

Why not ask if I'd like world peace. An end to hunger. A cure for cancer. Yes, absolutely! But I'm struggling to say something cool. Finally, master of bedroom dialogue that I am, I come up with this pearl: "Sure!"

It ain't Hemingway, but it gets her to slide down the bed.

Gwen isn't as skilled as Miranda, but she's working hard, and I'm responding in kind. We go from oral to something my former Commander-in-Chief would be forced to call sex. What Gwen lacks in experience, she makes up for with enthusiasm. I'm not getting every last ounce she's got to give, but I'm getting plenty. And just when she gets me to the very edge of ecstasy...

My cell phone rings.

It's a specific ring. I have four caller-specific ringtones, and I haven't heard this one in months.

"Damn it!" I say.

"Let it go, baby," Gwen says. "Tune it out. Keep riding the ride."

"I can't. It's my boss."

"Lucky?"

"It's my real boss."

"Make him wait. Call him back."

"You don't understand."

"You're right, I don't. I guess you'd better take the fucking call. It's not like you're doing anything important."

I stretch to reach for the phone, an act that disengages me from my lover faster than I'd like to admit.

"Asshole!" she says.

29.

"CREED, IT'S DARWIN."

"What's up?"

"I got a job for you."

I jump to my feet.

"When?"

"Now."

"Is it—"

"Important? Very."

Here's the thing about Darwin. He lets me do whatever I want, ninety-nine percent of the time. Even helps me by providing resources like body doubles, clean-up crews for people I kill, government airstrips, highest government clearance...you name it, I get it. But when he says something's important, it means one thing: the country's in danger.

"What do you need?"

By the time he tells me, Gwen is not only boiling mad, but completely dressed. I'm standing here naked, with the same handsome face she adored a few minutes ago, but I'm getting a vibe that our time here is done.

When I hang up she says, "Maybe I should be fucking him."

If what I suspect is true, that Gwen gets off on fucking men she perceives as powerful, then Darwin probably is the man for her. Then again, I've never laid eyes on him, so he could be

133

totally wrong for her. He could be anyone I run into on the street. Could be a woman, for all I know, since he uses voice altering equipment on the phone. In fact, Gwen is the only person I know who can't be Darwin, since I was with her just now while talking to him. Then again, you never know with Darwin.

"I need to take you home," I say, getting dressed.

"No. I'm going to buy an outfit. For tonight. I've decided I'll be in the mood when Maddie comes. And no, you can't watch. You'll have to listen from outside the locked door."

"I won't be there."

"What? Why not?"

"I have to leave town. It's urgent."

"You're supposed to be guarding me. I mean, us. What about Connor Payne?"

"That's what the phone call was about," I say, lying through my teeth.

"Connor Payne is your boss?"

"No, of course not. But my boss tracked him down. He's in San Francisco. I'm going there tonight. To kill him."

Her eyes widen. "No shit?"

I look into those wide, mud-brown eyes, and say, "I'm doing it for you, Gwen. I'm going to murder one of the most powerful men on earth. But first I'm going to punish him."

"Why?"

"Because he frightened you."

"Oh, Oh, wow!"

"I'm going to reduce him to tears."

"Oh, Oh, Oh, my God!"

"I'm going to make him shit his pants like a frightened child!"

"Oh! Oh! Oh! Oh, my God! Oh, Oh, my GOD!"

134

"And when he's on his knees, begging for his life, the last words he's going to hear before I snap his neck like a dead twig are, 'This is for Gwen.'"

"Oh! Oh! Oh! Oh, my God!" she screams. "Oh! Oh! Oh, my God! I'm getting wet!"

It's true. She's as worked up as anyone I've ever seen.

"Fuck me, Donovan! Fuck me! Fuck me right now!"

"There's no time."

From somewhere deep in Gwen's throat a moaning sound is born. By the time it escapes her lips, it is unlike any sound I've ever heard. Her eyes are half-closed, her head is lolling back and forth. Her hands are shaking.

"Donovan. Please! Oh God, I'm not kidding!"

She slaps my face as hard as I've ever been slapped.

"Fuck me!"

"I can't."

She slaps me again.

"Fuck me!

"Sorry."

"Fuck me! Now!"

She slaps me again.

"Right Now!"

And again.

I look at my watch. "I don't know…"

"Please!" She starts tearing her clothes off.

I'm bluffing about the time. I've got hours before I have to go save the world. This is all about coming at her the way I finally decided she wants to be fucked. And this time I guarantee I'm going to get every last ounce she has to give.

30.

"AFTER YOU KILL Connor Payne," she says.

"Yes?"

"Will I ever see you again?"

"Of course."

We're in my car, heading back to her place.

"When?"

"I'll be back before sunup."

"Swear to God?"

"Swear to God."

"Because Lucky owes you money?"

"No. You already told me he can't pay."

"I lied. He's got a million dollars in his safe."

I pause. "Why tell me that now?"

"Because I'm yours now. If you want me. And if we take Lucky's money, you won't have to support me."

"You'd leave him?"

"For you? Are you kidding me? Guy's a loser." She pauses a minute. "You do want me, right?" As if it never dawned on her I wouldn't.

The correct response in this situation is, Of course I want you! You're very important to me!—And I am going to say that.

In a minute.

But first I say, "You're a bit moody."

"I know, honey," she says. "But I don't have to be. I mean, I wouldn't be moody if I were with you."

"I'll require a lot of sex."

"Good thing I'm so young," she says. "By the time I stop liking sex, you'll be an old man."

"In that case, of course I want to be with you! You're very important to me."

"Really?"

"I swear."

I'm not lying. Gwen has become very important to me. Especially her titties. Because behind one of them, pressing against the edge of her rib cage, is the device. Phyllis implanted it during Gwen's boob job. I didn't see it, didn't feel it while making love just now, but I know it's there. Since it's ceramic, she's probably walked through a dozen airport scanners and no one ever knew. For Phyllis, it was the perfect place to hide the device, and the perfect way to get back at Lucky. Not to mention Gwen.

So yes, I want to be with Gwen. Want to protect her, keep her close at all times. At least till I recover the device. And maybe afterward, too, because Gwen has potential. She's smart, wild, and, once you know the combination, she's great in bed.

31.

AFTER DROPPING GWEN off I grab my gear and head to the private airstrip where I'll catch my flight. While driving there, I call Callie to invite her to come with me. She's been bored lately, and I know she'll jump at the chance to help me kill one of the FBI's highest-ranking terrorists. Unfortunately, Callie's cell phone has been turned off. Fortunately, it probably means she's having one of those incredible sexual gymnastic experiences with her life partner, Eva LeSage. Eva's a star in the most popular stage production in Las Vegas history. I've seen it twice, and paid money to see it the second time.

But I'd pay a fortune to see the show she and Callie put on behind closed doors!

Should I wait for Callie?

I know she'd love to come. And she's such a valuable asset, I'd be nuts not to wait for her. But the more I think about Darwin's plan, the less I like it. So I decide to go to San Francisco alone, and leave Callie behind to enjoy her evening with Eva.

In the air now, flying by private jet, I think about the job at hand. According to Darwin's intelligence, Rasool bin Muhaymin is due to land at San Francisco International Airport tonight at 10:19. Muhaymin, known to us as M, has been on the FBI's Ten Most Wanted Terrorists List for years.

He was indicted in the Southern District of New York for his role in the 2008 hijacking of a commercial airliner which resulted in the assault of twenty-four passengers and crew members, and the murder of three United States citizens. The Rewards for Justice Program has offered $5 million for information leading to M's apprehension or conviction in any country.

For apprehension or conviction, they say. Not for death.

Death makes more sense. Not just to me, but to Uncle Sam, as well. "Sam" knows our legal system is tiresome, cumbersome, expensive, and overly accommodating to high-profile defendants. So "Sam" (off the record) wants to handle M outside the courtroom. While the current charges against him are serious, M is far more dangerous than his indictment indicates. Simply put, Uncle Sam feels the world is better off without M, and when these things are decided from on high, I'm the one who gets the call.

Usually, I get to do things my way. This time, Darwin wants it done his way. Problem is, Darwin's plan sucks. He wants me to find the limousine that matches the license plate number he's provided. Then I'm to use whatever means necessary to take the limo driver's place. Once that's done, I'm to stand at baggage claim holding a sign that reads, Diego Santosch. M will get his bags and introduce himself to me as Diego, and I'll escort him to the limo. I'll put his bags in the trunk and open the door for him. When he crouches down to get in the car, I'm supposed to shoot him in the back of the head. I'll have the silencer attached, to reduce the sound. M will crumple into the rear seat, and I'll drive him to the pass-off person a few miles away.

It's so simple a hit man could do it.

And that's what bothers me.

Yeah, I know what you're thinking: I'm a hit man. Well, to the mob, maybe. But to Uncle Sam, I'm an assassin.

Big difference.

32.

THERE ARE LOTS of holes in Darwin's plan.

I like Darwin, enjoy working for him, but it's hard to trust a guy who would graft a kill chip to your brain. I mean, call me a bad sport, but it's not the sort of team-building exercise that inspires confidence.

For me, anyway.

So, in addition to worrying about a deadly terrorist, I have to worry that my own boss could be setting me up. I don't think he is, but isn't that when you're at the highest risk? When you think you're not?

It would be nice if:

1. Sensory could contact the limo company and tell them not to come. I could get my own limo, and wouldn't have to deal with the current driver. Except we can't contact the limo company because you never know who knows who. One of their employees could tip off M when he lands, and we could blow the opportunity to snuff him.

2. I could use my security clearance to wait for M at the gate, follow him to the bathroom, and kill him there. Except that M is too smart to use airport bathrooms.

3. I could wait on the jetway ramp. When M gets off the plane, I could hold him there and force him back on the plane after the passengers disembark. Then kill him and wait for a clean-up crew to remove the body. Except that M will certainly

be disguised, and it would be easy for him to slip past me on the jetway. Plus, he could be on a different flight.

4. I could board the plane before the passengers disembark, and ask the flight attendant where Diego Santosch is sitting. Except that M won't be flying under that name, and it won't appear on the passenger manifest. And again, he could be on a different flight.

There are other problems.

One is that the intelligence could be wrong, or at least faulty. I'm betting Darwin knows it's faulty. I mean, if you knew for certain M was on this particular flight, wouldn't you just isolate the plane on the tarmac and send a team out there to determine which passengers are not M and his followers? It wouldn't be hard to eliminate ninety percent of the passengers. Then you could arrest the other ten percent, and cull out the innocent with dental records and other manners of proof. What you're left with, over time, is M. Since the FBI is not doing that, I can safely assume they only think they know that M is on the 10:19 flight, that he's ordered a limo, and the driver will be waiting for him at the airport, holding a sign.

Or maybe Homeland knows about M being on the plane and hasn't shared the data with the FBI because they want him dead, not captured.

So many issues to consider. Want some more?

Who's to say M hasn't already landed? He could in fact already be at the airport, enjoying a drink, or having a leisurely dinner. He could be sitting in chairs at one gate after another, all afternoon, pretending to wait for various flights to board, and at ten tonight, he'll head to baggage claim to catch his ride.

He might not have any baggage to claim.

Another problem is the limo driver, who might not be a driver at all. What if he's an assassin? If he is, he could be working for them, us, or both. His job might be to kill me while I'm trying to find the limo. If I'm out in the limo parking lot looking for a license plate, and he's waiting for me, I'm a sitting duck.

Another problem is accomplices. What if M is traveling with others on the same flight? If someone sees me holding the sign at baggage claim and approaches me, how will I know for sure it's M?

Beyond all that, I don't like the idea of standing in baggage claim holding a sign that shows any possible double-crossers who to shoot.

There's only one way to sort these possibilities out. One way to successfully identify and kill the bad guy: I've got to put myself in M's shoes. If I'm M, I know the airport is my greatest point of vulnerability. If I'm M, I also know if I can get out of the airport, onto an interstate, it's game over. I win.

If I were M, how would I do it?

I think about it a few minutes, and come up with a foolproof plan for M.

Now all I have to do is come up with a plan to defeat it.

By the time I land, I've got one.

33.

IF I'M M, I'm already at the airport. I landed an hour ago, and I've got several hours to kill before my driver shows up. Instead of going to the main terminal, I surround myself with people by going from gate to gate, and sit among the crowds waiting to board the various planes. I sit at gate A12 for a half-hour, then go to A27 and read a book or check my emails. Then I go somewhere else. I'm not worried about my unclaimed luggage because I didn't check any. I've got a single bag that contains my laptop, a modest amount of cash, and a few articles of clothing. My cell phone is not only turned off, but the battery has been removed.

My three accomplices will be arriving, or have already arrived, on three separate flights. They also randomly move from gate to gate until we're all sitting at the same gate, waiting for a particular flight to land, probably around 9:45. We don't make eye contact or acknowledge each other in any way, but when the passengers exit the plane at this gate, the four of us merge with them and head to baggage claim.

The driver and limo company I've reserved are people I trust. Which means I have a way of knowing if the guy holding the sign is the right guy. He'll signal us that everything is okay, or if there's a problem. Something we've predetermined, such as which hand he holds the sign in, or if his other hand is in his pocket, if he puts on a hat, or whatever. Which means

Darwin's plan to use me as the limo driver wouldn't have worked.

But I already knew that.

If I'm M I have one of my accomplices approach the limo driver. The rest of us are at three different locations, with line of sight to the driver. If all goes well, Accomplice #1 and the driver get in the car and make a circle around the airport, and end up at passenger drop-off upstairs, where Accomplice #2 is waiting. He walks out the door and climbs into the limo. They drive away, get on the interstate, go a few miles, turn around and come back. I'm downstairs again, at baggage claim. When the limo driver comes in the door with a different sign, I walk past him and get in his car. While Accomplice #3 meets him at baggage claim, I drive the limo away, leaving the real driver and Accomplice #3 at the airport.

It's foolproof, because if at any point there's a problem, M can just walk out the door and catch a cab. He'd prefer not to, because the cab driver might be able to identify him later. Not a big deal, but still a loose end.

Now all I have to do is figure out which of the four is M.

Assuming I'm right about there being four.

Good thing I've got a plan for that. And for getting away after I shoot him.

34.

WHEN I LAND at the private airstrip in San Francisco, I assemble my gun, load it, and put it in my shoulder holster. I tape a strip of Velcro to the silencer, and tape two companion pieces to my left calf, under my pants leg. Then I attach the silencer to the strips. Later, I'll bring another strip of Velcro material to tape to my left arm, because if all goes right, this silencer will spend time in at least three different places over the next two hours.

I climb into the waiting cab and catch a ride to the airport. Once there, I find a quiet place to sit. Then I take off my jacket, spread it over my lap, and use it as a shield to hide my actions as I remove the silencer from my calf, and trust the Velcro to hold it in place underneath the chair.

Next I go to security, identify myself, and present my Connor Payne ID and security clearance papers. The folks at airport security escort me to the US Marshals' lounge, and give me the information I require, which is nothing more than telling me which luggage carousel the 10:19 plane will use to unload its baggage.

Carousel #6.

After I'm thoroughly patted down, vetted, and scanned, I request anonymity, explaining I'm on special assignment, testing baggage handling security. I tell them I don't want to be seen with any employees of the airport, or members of its security force. They have no problem with my requests, since my security clearance outranks all of them put together. They give me a special plastic security badge to wear around my neck in case someone tries to stop me, and a universal key card that allows access to the baggage handling areas. Then I start heading back to the seat where my silencer is hiding, and notice a kid jumping up and down on it. His mother is sitting across from him, completely oblivious. I've got the credentials to put a scare into both of them, but don't want to draw attention to the area, since I'll soon have a use for that silencer.

I work my way behind the scenes where the luggage to Carousel #6 will be unloaded in a couple of hours for the 10:19 p.m. flight. What I'm really looking for is an escape vehicle. I can't find one, so I call Lou Kelly and ask him to have a car and driver stationed behind the loading area to Carousel #6 at 10:15 tonight. When I come out, that car needs to be ready to go. I also need a military helicopter, and someone at the entrance gate who can make sure the gate opens when I'm ready to leave.

Twenty minutes later, Lou tells me the car, driver, and gate person will all be in place. The helicopter is a problem, since the area outside baggage service is a no-fly zone, as is the entire airport.

"It's an airport," I say. "How can it be a no-fly zone?"

"Only scheduled flights," he says. "You can't not know this."

"Well, schedule a flight."

"You can't schedule a helicopter flight to land in an airport baggage claim area. Why do you want one?"

"I want to create a diversion."

"Well, it won't be with a helicopter. But think it through. Do you really need a diversion? You've got the getaway car, the gate guy, and your private jet is less than a mile away."

"I need a diversion."

Lou sighs. "I'm open to suggestions."

"What about a bomb?"

"Excuse me?"

"A bomb is perfect," I say. "Much better than a chopper."

"A bomb."

"It's perfect, don't you see? Bombs freak people out. Especially in airports."

"You want me to find someone who's willing to bring a bomb into an airport. And then detonate it?"

"Yes, of course. And can you have him here within the hour?"

"You're joking."

"How long have we known each other?"

"What kind of bomb?"

"A loud one."

"A loud one," he says.

"Right. No damage, just noise."

"I'll let you know."

"Let me know before nine. That's when my phone goes dark."

35.

A COUPLE OF baggage guys ask about my security clearance. Not questioning it, just impressed. One woman is extremely suspicious. After giving me more attitude than Hop Sing gave the Cartwrights on *Bonanza*, she makes me stand by her desk while calling me in to the folks upstairs. When she hangs up her attitude is different. Now she wants to feel my biceps.

I head back to retrieve my silencer, and see that the boy who'd been jumping up and down on the chair has found it, and is blowing into it like a flute. Now he's chasing his sister around the area, trying to hit her over the head with it.

I need that silencer. It's essential to my plan. I don't understand why this family is sitting there. It's upstairs, by the check-in counter, where people sit while waiting for a wheelchair ride to the gate. They're taking up space that rightfully belongs to people who need help. Of the three, only the little girl seems normal. She's about three, and has the sense to stay away from her brother. The mom is large, and wearing some sort of shapeless patterned material. I know it can't be easy being a mom to a six-year-old criminal, but based on her demeanor, where she's sitting, her unkempt hair, lack of make-up, she's either given up, or never bothered to start.

I rush over to where the kid is starting to use my five-thousand-dollar state-of-the-art silencer as a hammer. I come up on him from behind. He winds up, intending to give it a huge, crushing blow against the chair arm, but I snatch it out of his hand and start moving away rapidly.

This event stirs the slumbering seed of motherhood that's been dormant in this woman since I began watching her. From some unknown pocket of flesh, or possibly her purse, she produces a whistle and blows it fit to bust. The boy is screaming and running after me in a fit of rage. The little girl laughs and claps her hands, thrilled to see her brother bested.

Security converges on me from all sides. I stop where I am, hand over my silencer, and tell them I need to take it with me to have it analyzed. They pass it around and it winds up in the hands of the US Marshal, who shows up with the head of airport security.

The whistling mom, her juvenile delinquent son, and normal daughter are standing with us. The mom is still blowing her whistle. The boy is yelling and kicking the shit out of my leg. I growl at him and he starts crying and hides behind his mother, which causes her to finally remove the whistle from her mouth.

"Did you see that?" she screams. "The bastard stole my son's toy, and now he's threatened his life! I want him arrested. Right now! I'm pressing charges!"

"Ma'am," the Marshal says. "This isn't your son's toy."

"Of course it is," she says. "I bought it at Wal-Mart yesterday. Cost me nearly twenty dollars."

He holds the silencer up so she can get a good look at it. "You're telling me this belongs to you?"

She says, "I bought it for my son. It's his. And I want it back."

They look at me. I shrug.

"I was trying to secure the weapon," I said. "I hadn't realized it was her weapon."

"Ma'am," the Marshal said. "You're going to have to come with me."

"What?"

"This is part of a weapon. You claim it's yours. Now we have to report it." To me he says, "Sorry, Agent Payne, but we're going to have to confiscate the silencer. It was found on airport property, and it's about to become evidence. We're going to have to keep it."

"Of course," I say. "Now that we know it's hers."

"Mine?" the woman says. "I thought it was the flute I bought my kid yesterday at Target."

"You said Wal-Mart," I pointed out, helpfully.

"You shut the fuck up!" she yells.

The Marshal holding the silencer says, "Come with me, ma'am. And if you blow that whistle again, I'm going to cuff you." They start walking away, so I start walking in the opposite direction.

"Agent Payne?" he calls out.

Shit. He probably wants to make me part of the paperwork. I turn around.

"Yes?"

"It just dawned on me that no one's thanked you for your vigilance. I appreciate your quick thinking. Sorry it only served to draw attention to you."

"No problem."

We continue walking in opposite directions. The mother is fussing loudly all the way to the door of the Marshals' lounge. I keep calling it a lounge, but there's also a small conference room in there, where the Marshals can get some work done while waiting for their next assignment. I turn to watch as they enter, and see the boy looking at me angrily. I stick my tongue out at him, and he gives me the finger.

Then I call Lou and order another silencer.

"I can't get one to fit your gun," he says. "Yours is custom."

"Then get me a new gun to go with it."

"That's easy. But the bomb's still a problem."

"Why?"

"I can't get anyone there in time that's not local. And the local guys won't detonate a bomb in their own airport."

"Will they bring me one?"

"Yes."

"Fine. Have them bring me the bomb, detonator, gun, and silencer."

"You up to handling all that by yourself?"

"Unless your guy wants to shoot the bad guys."

"I'd say you're on your own."

We work out the details for how the bomb guy will find me. It won't be easy, but I've established myself among the security folk, and should be able to pull it off.

36.

I THOUGHT ABOUT having the bomb guy simply walk in the front door and hand me the duffel. But even though I'm trusted by the security staff, watchful civilians might take note of the exchange, and report me. If that happens, someone will surely check the duffel, and I'll find myself crowded into the Marshals' lounge with my least favorite family.

So I've decided to have the bomb guy ride into the loading area with the getaway car driver. He'll wait for me there, show me how to detonate the charge, and I'll help him get through the security door and into the airport so he can catch a cab and be long gone before the action starts.

Lou and I confirm the timetable and synchronize our watches. Then I turn off my cell phone and remove the battery.

I've officially gone dark.

Now all I have to do is wait for the weapons to arrive. Then place the explosive. Then wait for the limo driver to show up with his sign. Then see if anyone approaches him. Then start shooting.

Are you beginning to understand the difference between a hit man and an assassin?

37.

I GRAB A burger, use the bathroom, check my watch. It's nine p.m. So much going on right now.

My weapons are about to arrive, but my mind is back in Vegas, where Lucky and Gwen are entertaining Maddie. Which means Gwen and Maddie are naked, doing whatever it is they do to each other while Lucky watches. I'm not sure how I feel about it. I'm a little jealous, I think, and more than a little muffed.

I mean miffed.

I pause, thinking about it. I'm going to go out on a limb and say Gwen won't participate. Not because I wore her out this afternoon, but because she and I have come a long way in the past day and a half. We've not only made a strong connection, we've also learned a great deal about each other.

And we've been intimate.

I might be wrong, and I know it's crazy early in our relationship, but—don't laugh—I believe she's starting to fall in love with me.

I know.

And brace yourself: I'm developing strong feelings for her.

I know what you're thinking: every time I sleep with a woman, I fall in love.

Well, you're right. I have no defense, other than to tell you

I only sleep with women who have a special effect on me. Yeah, I know. That sounds like horseshit, even to me.

I know what else you're thinking: every time I fall in love, something goes wrong. Sooner, not later.

True. But maybe this time things will be different.

I think about how alike we are, and how fate has brought us together. I mean, think about it: I've got a chip implanted in my brain, Gwen has a device implanted in her breast. My life is literally in her titty. You can't make this shit up.

I take a deep breath and decide that what's happening right now in Vegas needs to stay in Vegas, because I've got much more important things to worry about.

If my theory about M is correct, he and his accomplices have landed, and are sitting at the same gate at this very minute. I look at the escalator that leads to the hallway that leads to the gate terminals. People going up one side, heading to outbound flights, others coming down to claim their bags. If I'm right, the four terrorists are on the other end of that hallway. If I'm right, I'm within a mile of them.

If I'm right.

A cold chill of adrenalin surges through my veins, just thinking about it.

They're here.

I can feel them.

We're so close.

God, I'd love to snuff this bastard for you guys!

I can't go into details, but M is bad news. And he's got some very bad plans for you and your loved ones.

You've done nothing to him.

Nothing.

But he wants to hurt you anyway. Wants to maim and kill

your children.

We call him M, but as far as I'm concerned, it stands for motherfucker. And while I can't make you any promises, I'm going to do my best to send this bastard straight to hell tonight, and get him off your list of things to worry about.

38.

NINE-THIRTY.

My getaway car should be pulling up any second. But I don't see it.

…Nine-forty, still no car.

I can't just stand around here forever. Soon M's limo driver will walk into baggage claim with his sign. He'll be located one floor up, near the carousel I'm watching from below.

It's busy out here. People are working hard all around me. Baggage cars come and go, hooked together, three, four, five at a time, like little trains. They deliver the bags that come from all over the world to people standing impatiently right above us. It's astounding, really, when you think about it. People bitch and moan about losing this bag or that, but when you're out here among these hard-working men and women, you realize the enormity of what they're trying to accomplish. Sure they make the occasional mistake. Who doesn't? But these people are amazing! If they weren't on a strict timeline, they'd have a 100 percent delivery rate. As it is, they're within shouting distance of it. What strikes me is the bags never stop moving! It's a nice, clear night, but I know these guys work just as hard when it's cold, raining, or snowing.

Wait. Strike that. It doesn't snow in San Francisco. But it does get cold. Someone once said, "The coldest winter I ever spent was one summer in San Francisco!" It is, in fact, the coldest major city in America during the summer months. As for baggage people in other parts of the country who work through snow and ice and rotten weather?

I love 'em.

But I digress.

I know I'm rambling, and it's not because I'm nervous. It's just that I'm standing here watching hundreds of bags being delivered every minute, while my people—who are supposed to be the best in the world—can't bring me a simple bomb, gun, silencer, and some bullets.

I just want my stuff.

So I can do my job.

Is that too much to ask?

Nine-fifty. No car, no duffel.

I don't have to use a silencer. I can shoot the bad guys perfectly well with the gun in my shoulder harness.

But it'll make a lot of noise, and everyone will see me. So, yeah, a silencer would be great. And a small, loud bomb to detonate, away from the action, so everyone will look that way when it's time for me to haul ass. Speaking of things that would be great, let's don't underestimate the value of a getaway car. I'd love to kill the bad guys and get away without being shot or killed.

All these things would be great to have.

But they're not necessary.

And they're not necessary because killing M is worth dying for. It is, in fact, a good exchange, because I can only kill a few dozen terrorists in my life, while he can kill thousands of Americans.

I wonder briefly if Lou even bothered to get me a car. I don't want to whine, or dwell too much on what it's like working every day with people I don't trust. I mean, you might have it ten times worse than me at your job. When I tell you my boss gave me a new face against my wishes, you might say, "You think that's bad?" and you might have a worse story. Lou, the guy I rely on to help me take down the bad guys, tried to kill me and steal all my money a few months ago. And might be trying to kill me tonight, by denying me a getaway car. But you might have a coworker that makes Lou look like a choirboy.

I don't like to make assumptions about Darwin and Lou. But Darwin's plan would almost certainly have gotten me killed tonight. Is that what he intended?

No way to know. Darwin's a company guy, ruthless as a slumlord who knows about the gold filling in your tooth. But far as I know, he's never worked in the field. Maybe he's just a bad planner.

I glance at my watch for the fifth time in ten minutes.

It's time.

I have to go upstairs, take a position from which to survey the scene.

I've got a plan.

I'll make it work.

I start walking toward the security door. While I walk, I scan the endless concrete around me...

...And see a black sedan entering the far gate.

39.

THE SEDAN PULLS up and I meet the driver and have him back into the space I've reserved. The folks in baggage are comfortable with me, and when I tell them I'm escorting a dignitary out the back they're more excited than suspicious. The local guy who brought me the bomb turns out to be a kid of twenty-two, who looks like he's about to faint.

"Relax, son," I say. "I'll get you out of here."

"Yes, sir."

I pause for a moment. I have to wonder if maybe the reason he's so nervous is because he's got the real detonator in his pocket, and plans to blow me up when he walks out the front door. I shake my head, trying to rid myself of the paranoia.

Still...

I lean him and the driver up against the car and pat them down like my life depends on it. Then I apologize, and let the driver get back in his car. The kid and I climb in the back seat. I tell him to show me his bomb, and explain how it works. It's dark, so I flip on my pen light and train it on the floor. There's just enough glow to see what he's holding. As I instructed, he's placed the bomb in a soft drink cup that has a plastic lid on it, and a straw sticking out. The straw holds the antenna for the receiver. He hands me the detonator, which is the size of a garage-door opener, and has two buttons.

"What's the second button for?"

"Press either one. They both work."

"Why have two?"

He shrugs. "It's my garage-door opener. It came that way."

Now I'm starting to get a little nervous.

"What's the range for detonating it?"

"Sixty yards."

"The trash can is metal."

"So?"

"Want to change your range estimate?"

"Nope."

"That's a pretty bold statement," I say, "for someone who hasn't seen the trash can yet. What are you basing the distance on?"

"Educated guess."

"A guess," I repeat.

"Yes, sir."

"And have you tested the range before?"

"Of course."

"In a metal trash can?"

"No."

"So you don't even know if it will detonate."

"Oh, it'll detonate, all right!" he says, enthusiastically.

I may have doubted the kid at first. But now I believe him. I like a guy who loves his work.

"And the bomb is safe?" I say.

"Define safe."

"Big bang, no injuries."

"Where's the opening on the can?"

"There's a round hole on the top, maybe a foot in diameter."

"When you detonate it, make sure no one's leaning over the top."

"Because?"

"The explosion's going to shoot up about ten feet."

"But nothing through the sides?"

"No. It's a noise bomb. And smoke. I assumed you wanted smoke."

"Smoke is good."

"If there's paper in the trash can, it'll ignite."

"They can deal with that later."

I put the garage-door detonator in my pocket and say, "Show me the gun and silencer."

He opens the duffel enough so I can look inside. I reach in and heft it.

Feels right.

I use my pocket knife to cut a hole in the duffel bag large enough to accommodate the barrel of the silencer. Then push the barrel through the hole about an inch, and cover that part of the duffel with my jacket. I keep the top of the duffel unzipped, so I can reach in and shoot when the time comes, without having to brandish the gun.

"Ready?" I say.

"Can't wait to get out of here," he says.

I hand the kid his soft drink bomb and say, "Pretend to sip from the straw while we walk through baggage handling. When we get to the steps, you take the lead. Walk through the door at the top of the steps, go thirty yards to the trash can. Stand there a few seconds, pretend to take one last sip, then drop it in the trash. Don't make eye contact with anyone. After dumping the container, you're free to go out the front door, catch a cab, and go wherever you like. If the bomb works I'll send you some serious cash as a token of my appreciation. Any questions?"

"No sir."

When he climbs the steps and walks out the door, I turn

and retrace my steps back out the door and walk a hundred yards to a second entrance, climb those steps and backtrack toward Carousel #6, with the duffel over my shoulder. I'll walk there like any other passenger who's landed and is waiting for luggage.

40.

THE FIRST THING I see upon entering the main baggage claim area is a line of limo drivers, all of whom are holding signs. I scan them as I walk by, but don't see the name Diego Santosch. Good thing, since M's driver shouldn't be in this area.

Just beyond the rental car kiosks, I come to Carousel #6. I take up my position by the conveyor belt on the far side, next to the opening where the baggage exits.

A dozen men and women are standing around, waiting for bags from the previous flight. I glance at my watch. M's flight should be arriving in twelve minutes. I'm positive he's not on it, but don't see anyone in the vicinity of Carousel #6 who I'd profile as a possible terrorist.

More people wander into the area. Most position themselves near the baggage entrance. A few gather at the middle. No one is standing near me. A few more people drift in. Among them is a well-dressed man in a suit, holding a sign at his side. I'm sure this is the driver. The fact he hasn't lifted the sign tells me he knows M hasn't arrived in the area yet. That doesn't mean he knows M. It could simply mean he knows the flight hasn't arrived yet.

Five minutes pass, and now there are thirty people standing around the conveyor belt. One lady walks past the others and takes up a position fifteen feet from me, and turns around to face the baggage entrance door. She's foreign, but I can't place her nationality based on the quick glance I got.

Suddenly I spot two men that could be my targets. One standing at the center of the conveyor, where it makes a half-circle, the other looking around, as if trying to find a porter to help with his luggage.

Only he doesn't seem to notice the porter standing near the rental car kiosk a mere thirty feet away.

If something's going to happen, I hope it's now, because the area's not too crowded yet, and I have clear sight lines to the driver.

I'm looking at the driver, and the guy who's looking around. The driver puts his right hand in his pocket, and holds the sign up with his left hand. I focus on the hand in his pocket. He's holding something that could be a small gun. The guy who's being far too obvious about looking around suddenly notices the sign and holds up his hand. He walks over to the driver, who lowers the sign but keeps his hand in his pocket.

This isn't going down the way I expected. The two of them are standing there, making small talk. More people are heading toward Carousel #6. Dozens of them. If I wait much longer, I won't have a clear shot.

I don't know what M looks like, but I'm positive the guy standing by the driver isn't him. I'm also positive the driver is holding a gun in his right pocket. As the people are about to overtake our carousel, I glance at the trash can to make sure there's no one within fifteen feet of it. There's not.

But where's M?

Where the fuck is M?

I have to do something.

I put my hand in the duffel, turn slightly, and shoot the

driver. The face of the guy standing next to him registers shock as he sees blood squirting from the driver's chest. He turns and looks at me. I shoot him, and pause a split second, then fire two shots at the foreign lady whose back is to me. Both shots slam into the base of her skull. The impact spins her around, and she lands on her back. As it registers through the crowd that three people are on the floor, bleeding, I run toward the lady, as if attempting to offer help. At the same time I reach into my pocket for the detonator. As I get to her, I press the button, and the trash can explodes. People everywhere are screaming and ducking for cover. No one is looking in my direction. Standing over the lady, I shoot her point blank between the eyes, turn, and run through baggage exit, down the conveyor belt, out the door, and into the car.

41.

THE DRIVER LOU hired is very good.

Seconds later, he's got us through the gate, racing toward my private jet. Ten minutes after that, I'm on board. I want to call Callie, have her turn on the TV and let me know what's happening. But I can't use my cell phone to do it, since I don't trust Lou or Darwin not to home in on my signal with a surface-to-air missile. For this reason I only use my cell on planes when we're above 20,000 feet. As the engines start firing, I try calling Callie using the onboard flight phone, but amazingly, her phone is still dark.

I think about calling Gwen, but decide against it. I don't know what the TV announcers are saying, or if I've been videoed on someone's cell phone. I wouldn't want her to get the wrong opinion about me. I mean, the right opinion. I also don't want to tip Lucky off to our relationship until I'm there to protect her. I don't think he'd be stupid enough to hit her, but why give him the chance to consider it?

I call Lou.

"You made the news," he says.

"Me?"

"They're looking for Connor Payne. He's a person of interest in the airport attack."

"What're they saying?"

"That he's a foreign agent who breached security. Had

phony papers that gave him top-level security clearance."

"What's the government say?"

"Never heard of him."

"Typical."

"What happened?" Lou says.

"What are they reporting?"

"Three people dead, twenty-three wounded."

"Wounded?"

"Stampede. Apparently a bomb went off. People freaked."

"Anyone seriously injured?"

"Not that I've heard."

"Thank God for that. Hang on a sec."

The co-pilot turns to me and motions me to end the call.

"We're taking off," I say. "Call you later."

When we pass 20,000 feet, I put the battery back in my cell phone and see that Callie has called me twice, and Darwin has called five times. My phone buzzes. I check the caller ID. Make that six times.

"Where are you?" he snaps.

"Airborne."

"You never made contact with the limo driver. Why?"

"He knew them."

He pauses. "How do you know?"

"Several reasons. In addition to those, he had a gun in his pocket. I don't suppose you know anything about that, do you?"

"Of course I do."

"Really?"

"He was one of ours."

"Ours?"

Uh oh.

I ask, "Have you heard from him?"

168

"No, asshole. You killed him, remember?"

"Who told you?"

"Marshals Service. What do you mean he knew them?"

"When he recognized one of them, he put his right hand in his pocket, where his gun was. Then he raised the sign with his left hand."

"That doesn't prove anything."

"You weren't there. Trust me, he knew them."

He pauses.

"I thought he might. That's why we put him there."

"Excuse me?"

"I wanted to see how you'd handle it. Figured you'd kill him if he deserved to die."

"You had me assassinate one of our guys?"

"I didn't make you pull the trigger. Why did you, by the way? And how did you know M was dressed like a woman?"

"The driver knew the accomplice, but not M. The accomplice knew M and the driver. I figured if I shot the driver suddenly, without sound or warning, the accomplice would instinctively turn to look at M. I was right. He looked directly at the woman in front of me. Couldn't take his eyes off her. Looked nowhere else. It had to be M."

"So you shot her."

"Him."

"What if you'd been wrong?"

"I'd feel terrible."

"But you'd get over it."

"I never get over it. But I move along."

Darwin pauses a long time before speaking. At no time does he thank me for a job well done, or congratulate me, or say anything to make me feel wanted, needed, or appreciated. Doesn't even give me the reassurance he isn't plotting to kill me. When he speaks, he's curt.

"I'll call you when I need you," he says.

And that's that.

Take off to landing is eighty-three minutes, according to the onboard display panel. I spend most of it talking to Lou. I probe him about Darwin, to see if he's got an opinion about what happened. He says all the right things, but who knows what he, or Darwin, or both of them might be up to? I tell him to send twenty grand to the nervous kid who made the bomb, and add it to my bill.

"We were lucky to find him on such short notice," Lou says.

"Keep him on the payroll. The kid knows his bombs. What's his name?"

"Joe Penny."

"Good kid," I say.

"I'll tell him you said so."

We hang up and I think about what Darwin asked. How would I feel if I'd shot an innocent woman in the back? Thinking about it now, I can't imagine I took a chance like that. But at the time, when I was in the moment, it seemed obvious.

And maybe that's the real difference between a hit man and an assassin.

42.

I'M IN THE rental car, heading to Lucky's house.

I called Gwen after landing, but got no answer. I thought about leaving a message, but I'm the world's worst when it comes to voicemail. If Gwen isn't waiting up to let me in I'll sleep in the car. In fact, I'll sleep in the car anyway, and make Lucky happy.

This guy Lucky never warmed up to me after I threatened to kill him. Nor was he thrilled I made Hampton Hill feel him up. Nor will he be pleased to learn I spent two hours fucking his wife instead of guarding him. Hell, when Gwen and I run off together he'll probably be upset about that, too.

It's like my grandpa often said: "There's just no pleasing some people."

I'm a mile away from Lucky's when I realize something is terribly wrong up ahead. The road is flat, the horizon full of colors. The kind of colors cop cars and ambulances make.

The line of cop cars starts a hundred yards before Lucky's gates, and continues fifty yards beyond. There are a dozen cars in Lucky's front yard, and at least two ambulances. Though it's after midnight, there's traffic, and it's crawling as people crane their necks to gawk. Two cops are directing, telling everyone to move along. I want to say something, but can't. If I ask what's happened, the cops'll tell me to move along. If I tell them I'm Lucky's bodyguard, all hell will break loose. They'll want to know where I was, what I was doing, who was I with, why wasn't I here, and of course, I'll become their primary suspect. They'll start looking into my past and see I have none. This will raise eyebrows and next thing you know, I'm in lock-up.

What's the best thing that can happen at that point? That someone in San Francisco took my picture on their cell phone and will help me establish an alibi? That I won't be in trouble for whatever happened at Lucky's because I was busy setting off a bomb and killing people in San Francisco?

No thanks.

As I slowly pass Lucky's entrance, I stop as long as I can and crane my neck, same as all the others did. Except that I'm looking for Lucky and Gwen among the two dozen people talking and taking pictures around the gate, in the yard, and around the house. I don't see either of them, but I do see two large blankets covering two large bodies next to the gates. My best guess is someone killed the gate goons, and Lucky called the cops.

I don't think Lucky and Gwen are hurt, because if someone planned to kill them, they'd have to kill the gate goons first. You say obviously they did, but I say why leave them lying on the ground? If, after killing the gate goons, you still had to kill Lucky and Gwen, wouldn't you drag the bodies out of plain sight before approaching the house?

I would.

So I'm not overly concerned about Mr. and Mrs. Peters.

I keep moving.

After passing Lucky and Gwen's house, I keep driving until I find a little L-shaped neighborhood shopping center that has a sports bar. Business isn't booming, but the joint's not empty, either. I find a parking place, go inside, and belly up to the bar.

The bartender's busy, but he nods, and I take it to mean I'm next on his list.

"You come from the town side?" he says.

I nod. "Any idea what happened?"

"From what they're sayin'..." he gestures to one of the TVs. "It's four people dead. All of 'em shot execution style." He goes on to explain what that means: "Once in the chest, once in the head."

I don't care what he's saying. I'm suddenly in a daze.

"Four people?"

"That's what they're sayin'." He digs some ear wax out of his ear with his little finger, inspects it, then flicks it at the empty space between me and the grizzled drunk who's sitting two stools down from me.

"Hey, Benny!" he shouts at the small group crowded around another TV.

A young guy with a beard and a faded blue work shirt turns around.

Bartender says, "What's the latest?"

Young guy says, "Which one? Airport or Lucky Peters?"

Bartender looks at me. "You hear about the airport?"

"Yeah."

Bartender nods and yells, "Peters! They identify the bodies yet?"

"They think it's him and his wife, and two bodyguards."

"Have they made a positive ID yet?" I ask.

"Dunno. Want a drink?"

"It's a bar, right?"

"It's the only bar, three miles, every direction."

"Then I'll have whatever your best bourbon is."

"Water, ice, twist?"

"Are you shitting me?" I growl.

He stares at me.

"Straight up," I say.

With a heavy heart I toss the bourbon down my throat and join the group huddled around the TV broadcasting news instead of ball games.

"They're showin' pictures of Lucky and Gwen Peters," one of them says as I pull up a stool.

"Anyone here know them?" I say.

They look around at each other.

"Just heard of Lucky, is all," the young guy with the work shirt says. "You?"

"Nope."

The cameras are live, at Lucky's house. On the screen, they superimpose several photos. There's a shot of Lucky accepting some sort of giant check. Next, a shot of the vacant lot with a giant sign that says Vegas Moon. Next, a photo of Lucky and Gwen, taken at their Vegas church wedding a few months ago. She's wearing the same cut-off jeans she had on earlier today. Or yesterday, or whenever it was. She's got one foot on the floor, other in the air showing off the white lace garter on her thigh. One of the guys says, "Now that there is one fine piece of ass."

My mood is so foul, had he insulted her, I would've killed him.

43.

CARMINE "THE CHIN" Porrello is hard of hearing, I decide, based on the sound coming from the speakers in his theater room. He's so busy watching the Lucky Peters drama unfold, he doesn't even notice me standing behind him.

Until he does.

"What the fuck?"

Carmine's in his early seventies, barrel-chested, with thin arms and wispy gray hair. He appears to have more hair coming out of his ears, nose and underwear than he has on his head.

I take the seat to his left. It's a couple feet closer to the screen, and the angle isn't as good as his. But it's a perfect spot for me to keep an eye on him and the door behind him at the same time.

Carmine isn't happy I'm in his home. On the other hand, he's still alive. He recovers quickly, as tough guys usually do.

"Pour you a drink?" he says.

"No. I'm good."

"I'm still alive," he says. Then adds, "How come?"

"I want some answers."

"Any old answers? Or do I gotta tell the truth?"

He laughs until he sees I'm not laughing. Then he stops.

"I'm willing to overlook the disrespect," he says. "If you do two things."

Normally I wouldn't let him try to establish control like that, but I'm busy deciding how I want to kill him. Do I want to mince his flesh and set him on fire? Hammer nails into his head? Cut off his nuts, sew them in his mouth, and tickle his ass with a feather? So many choices.

He clears his throat. "I said…"

"I don't care what you said, Carmine. It's what you say next that matters."

He starts to say something, but I raise an eyebrow. He changes his mind and says, "Whadya wanna know?

44.

"TELL ME EVERYTHING you know about Gwen. And don't say Gwen who."

Carmine nods. "Helluva girl, that one."

I wait.

He says, "Fuckin' pity. Swear to God, I find out who clipped her, I'll kill 'em with my bare hands."

I say nothing in response, show nothing in my expression. What I'm thinking is Carmine's got a huge head. I wonder how much gasoline it would hold.

"Unless it was you that killed 'em," he says. "In which case I figure they had it comin'."

I don't speak.

Carmine says, "Heard you was bodyguardin' Lucky. Figured you wouldn't of taken that job less you was workin' some kind of angle. Maybe you found a way to take over his business?"

Carmine waits for me to respond, but gets nothing.

He says, "God knows I tried."

Then he says something that completely floors me: "How'd you find out Gwen was workin' for me?"

45.

"YOU DIDN'T KNOW?"

"No."

"Shit."

"Let's hear it."

Carmine says, "Can I turn that fuckin' TV down?"

He reaches for the remote, presses the mute button. Says, "My wife's asleep. If she wakes up and comes in to check on me, you won't make her a part of this, will you?"

"She won't be joining us tonight."

Carmine's face goes white. Well, whiter.

"Relax," I say. "I just pennied her into the room."

"What's that mean?"

"I pressed a couple of coins into the door jamb. She won't be able to open her door until someone removes the coins. If she starts banging the door, you'll know she's awake."

"Oh. Thanks."

"You said Gwen was working for you."

"Right." He clears his throat. "Okay, it's clear you've become, ah, ah..."

"Close to her."

"Right."

"So?"

"So you gotta understand, anythin' I tell you happened before you and her ever met. And I don't know shit about what happened these last few days."

He pauses.

I say, "Don't make me ask you again."

"Right. Well, Gwen was on my payroll. I hired her to, ah, seduce Lucky. Well, she done it so well he up and asked her to marry him after a few fuckin' weeks! So I give her permission, 'cause I want her to get me names, numbers, point spreads... you know, the works."

I wait for him to continue.

"Well, she gets me nothin'. I mean, the motherfucker is locked up tighter than Fort Knox. I think she's lyin' at first, so I threaten her a bit." He looks at me and quickly adds, "No physical stuff. Just angry talk. You know."

He looks at me, sees I'm not participating. Continues. "So anyway, I'm increasin' the pressure on her, you know, turnin' the screws, and then you come into the picture. Now I want no part of it, so I tell her I'm done, have a good life."

He shakes his head. "And now this."

I think about how Gwen asked me how much to kill Lucky. How much to kill Carmine. Now I know why. Carmine doesn't like the way I'm looking at him.

He says, "I know this makes me look bad."

"Ya think?"

"Let me tell ya somethin'," he says. "I've known this girl since the first time she got knocked up."

I sigh. "Go on."

"When she turned eighteen she started dancin' for me."

"By dancing, you mean?"

"In the strip clubs."

I sigh again. Deeper, this time.

"That's where she met Lucky," Carmine says. "You really didn't know this?"

"Just out of curiosity," I say, "what was her stage name?"

"You don't know?"

"I asked you, didn't I?"

"Didn't matter which club she danced," Carmine says, "her stage name was always the same: Vegas Moon."

46

"I'M GOING TO ask you just once," I say.

"Did I kill her? No. Did I have her killed? No. Would I kill her?"

I arch my brows.

He pauses a minute, then says, "Yeah. I would've. If she stole from me."

"And did she?"

"She was paid to get me information. After she married a millionaire, and didn't deliver the goods, I felt a reimbursement was due."

"How much?"

"Fifty, give or take."

I look at this old warrior and see a grandfather lying on a reclining theater chair, wearing a housecoat and slippers. His housecoat's been open the whole time I've been here, his old man underwear showing, and he never even noticed. This was and is one of the most feared men in the country. Carmine "The Chin" Porrello, a man who once boasted he could lift his chin and cause the death of ten men.

And his underpants are showing.

He was and is one of the most ruthless mob bosses in the history of the mob, and his nuts are hanging out of his tighty-whities, along with a thatch of coarse, gray hair.

Some Indian tribes used to believe if you killed a powerful

man, his power would add to yours. I doubt that's true, but as with all things Native American, it wouldn't surprise me, either. What does surprise me is Gwen working as a stripper for Carmine Porrello for two years, and taking money from the mob to marry Lucky. I mean, I've heard of women getting lucky, and women marrying for money. But this story takes it to a whole new level.

I think about it awhile, and realize none of this matters. And the reason it doesn't matter is because, like Carmine said, it's history. Okay, so she stripped in a club for a couple of years. Got knocked up a few times. Was part of the mob. Married a man she didn't love. Took money to steal his secrets. Got off on fucking hot lesbians and powerful men.

But which of us is perfect?

I liked her. Might have even been able to love her, given the right opportunity.

"What happens now?" Carmine says.

What indeed?

My cell phone vibrates.

It's Callie.

47.

"I TRIED TO call you," she says. "Several times."

"I know. I had to go dark."

"I figured that out when I turned on the TV."

"I tried to call. Wanted to take you with me."

I look at Carmine. He waves at me like, Go ahead, don't mind me. Please, finish your call.

"I turned off my phone," Callie says.

"I know. But it was off longer than I expected."

"I followed her."

I think a minute, then realize she's talking about her life partner, Eva LeSage. I remember Callie telling me she'd put a tracking device in Eva's car.

"What happened?" I say.

"I followed her to someone's house."

I get a cold chill.

Callie says, "Lucky Peters'. I passed by a couple of times, tried to call you, see what you wanted me to do…" her voice trails off.

"And then?"

"I snapped."

"Define snapped."

"I killed the gate guards, broke in the front door, followed the music to the bedroom. Kicked in the door, saw Eva fucking Lucky."

"Where was…" I look at Carmine. I don't want to say Gwen's name.

"Gwen?"

"Yeah."

"She was there, too."

I close my eyes.

"I'm sorry, Donovan. I couldn't help it."

"Give me five minutes."

"You coming over? Or calling me back?"

"Both."

"Should I arm myself?"

"No. Of course not."

She pauses.

I say, "You don't trust me?"

She says, "Do you trust me?"

I think about it a few seconds. And a few seconds more. "Yes."

"Thanks, Donovan."

"And you?"

"Do I trust you?" she says.

"Yes."

"No."

"Figures."

I hang up.

Carmine says, "If that was good news, you haven't notified your face."

"The news was bad for me, good for you," I say.

"Sorry. Sort of."

"I don't have it on me," I say, "but I'll see that you get your money back."

"What money?"

"The fifty grand Gwen owes you."

He looks at me with surprise. "She's alive?"

"No. But I don't want her memory tarnished."

Carmine looks at me with what might be tears in his eyes. "You're a good man. I think if you pay me the fifty Gs, I won't have you killed."

I look into his tear-stained eyes and say, "I'll pay you a hundred if you promise to try."

He does a double-take.

"What kind of crazy fuckin' guy are you?" he says.

"How about it?"

"Fuck no! Just give me the fifty and get the fuck outta my life. No disrespect."

48.

"YOU FOUND EVA fucking Lucky," I say, while driving toward Callie's.

"Did you know it was going on?"

"Of course not. I mean, Gwen said a woman named Maddie came over from time to time. But I had no idea it was Eva."

"How long had it been going on?"

"I don't know. A few months at most."

"Where did they meet?"

"I don't know. I don't know anything more than I've told you, except that Gwen used to participate. When she was in the mood."

Neither of us speaks for a minute. I listen to the sound my tires make as they roll over tar patches on the road.

Finally I say, "Tell me what happened."

"I left the guards out front, knew I didn't have much time. Eva started begging for her life. She was naked, on her knees, head bowed…it was pitiful. But I was furious, you know?"

"I know."

I also know that Callie never leaves any loose ends. If she killed Eva, she killed Lucky. And if she killed Lucky, she killed Gwen. Callie never leaves anyone alive who can identify her.

She'd kill the fucking rooster, if she thought it could talk.

"You executed Eva," I say.

"Eventually."

"Eventually?"

"After I stopped laughing."

"You laughed?"

"She looked so ridiculous! I don't know, Donovan. When you're not part of the sex, it all looks so...silly."

"On the news it said they found four bodies."

"Right."

"You took Eva with you."

"No. I wanted the world to see what she was doing. And the pig she was doing it with."

"What did you do to Gwen?"

"You're going to be very angry."

49.

"WHAT DID YOU do to Gwen?" I repeat.

"How close were you? Had you already fallen in love?"

"We were as close as two people can become in the space of a day."

"You know how absurd that sounds, don't you?"

"Story of my life. Look, I'm not mad at you. You mean... everything to me. We go way back. I've already lost Quinn, lost Lou for all practical purposes, can't trust Darwin. You're all I have. And even you don't trust me."

She sighs. "If I knew you were going to make a speech I would've made popcorn."

"Funny."

"Cut to the chase, Donovan."

"I really cared about her. But there's more."

"Tell me."

"You remember the device I've been looking for?"

"Of course."

"I'm certain Phyllis buried it in one of Gwen's implants."

"What?"

"When she did her boob job."

Callie laughs. "That's hilarious! What a perfect way to get back at her and Lucky."

"You understand it?"

"I'm a woman, remember?"

"I do."

"And now you want to recover the device."

"If I can. Where's Gwen's body?"

"In the trunk of my car."

"I'll be there in five."

"I'll meet you in the garage."

The last five minutes of my drive to Callie's were difficult. I'm a Time Saver, a person who captures special moments in his life, stores them in his brain, and can replay them with precision. I didn't take the time to properly save my moments with Gwen these past couple of days. In truth, I didn't know how special they were going to be. So, for the next few minutes, I focus on the highlights.

I think about the first time I saw her wearing that silly pink T-shirt that said Eat Me! if you read it a certain way. I smile, thinking about Fast Eddie and his plastic wife, Surrey, and how Gwen schooled me about the odds she'd memorized. I'll keep the memory of how she called Lucky a bullshit artist. I'm sad, now, thinking about her look of despair when Eddie told Hampton to be gentle, because the money was more important to him than her dignity. I'll never forget the look it put in Gwen's eyes. I know I'll disappoint my share of women over the course of my life. But I'll never give a woman cause to show me a look like the one I saw on Gwen's face when Hampton tried to make his move. I think about that some more, and feel that twitch I get sometimes before bad things happen. It's at this moment I think I'll kill Hampton on my way out of town, after burying Gwen on the vacant commercial lot, right smack under the sign that says Vegas Moon. Named after me, Gwen had said, and now I know why.

I'm going to be buried there someday, she'd said. And you have to respect my dying wish.

I will respect it, sweetheart.

I'll have her cremated, then I'll dig a trench under the sign while Callie stands guard. I'll sprinkle Gwen's ashes in it, say a few words, and fill the hole back in with my hands. I'll kiss the ground that covers her, too.

I think about how Gwen gave me lukewarm sex the first time, and hot, wild, monkey sex after deciding I had enough power to kill the mob boss that was threatening her. The look on her face when she had to have it is something I'll never forget. I'm smiling now, thinking about it. And the sex that final time? Let me just say this: could a man possibly die a better death than from getting the best sex a woman can give? If you say yes, I'm happy for you. But keep it to yourself. No, strike that. I want to hear what you come up with. Whatever it is, I'll take Gwen and give you odds: 2,000 to 1.

A block from Callie's place, I pull to the side of the road and stop a minute. I need a memory to help me wrap all these scattered images into a tidy little package so I can label it in my mind, under Gwen.

And then it hits me.

The one image that stands above the rest: when Gwen and I walked her rooster down that long driveway!

I remember how she got angry when I asked if it crowed every morning. I realize now she wasn't angry about the stereotyping of the rooster. She was living a huge stereotype, and didn't like it, and was attempting to change her life around.

I think about Gwen and her rooster, and the leash, and the harness she tied it to.

There's one problem with the image: I don't like the outfit she was wearing. When we did the cock walk, she had on gray sweatpants and that silly pink T-shirt. Later that evening, she wore the black sweater with the sleeves rolled up to just above the elbows, tucked into a black, pleated skirt. She also had on a pair of fire-engine-red boots with a black heel and two rhinestone strips attached over the toe, and above the upper ankle. I remember the boots stopped mid-calf, and left plenty of leg showing.

It's my memory, right?

I can save it any way I choose.

I close my eyes, think of her evening outfit, and superimpose it over the cock walk outfit.

Wait—am I boring you with all this? If so, back up and rethink it. If you're not saving the precious memories in your life, what the hell are you going to have when you're locked away in a maximum security cell some day, waiting to be executed?

I superimpose the one outfit over the other, and what goes into the memory box is this: a gorgeous woman walking a rooster down her driveway, while wearing one of the hottest outfits I've ever seen.

I close my eyes, lock the memories in my mind, and think, I'm going to miss you Gwen. And everything we might have become.

50.

CALLIE'S HOLDING A gun on me.

We're in the garage of her condo. Five of the six indoor parking places have cars in them. Only Eva's spot is empty. It's quiet as a tomb in here, and musty. As I walk toward her I hear my footsteps echo off the concrete walls and ceiling. She lifts the barrel of her gun slightly, to indicate I'm close enough. I stop twelve feet from her.

"Either shoot me or open the trunk," I say.

"Show me your hands."

I do.

She pulls a fillet knife from her handbag and places it on the rear bumper of her car.

"What's that for?"

"You wanted the device, right?"

"Jesus, Callie."

She takes a few steps back, then pops the trunk. At first it takes my eyes some time to adjust to what I'm seeing. Because what I see is something I'm not prepared for.

Gwen's alive.

She's got a hood over her head, and her wrists and ankles are bound with shipping tape, and she's obviously unconscious, because she's not making a sound. But she's very much alive. I can tell because one of her legs is twitching. As is her head.

I look at Callie. "What's going on?"

"I couldn't get in touch with you."

"So?"

"So after taking one look at her I said, 'Are you fucking Creed?'"

"And she said?"

"Yes. I love him."

"She said that?"

"She did."

"And you spared her?"

"I figured you'd want to say goodbye before I killed her."

"But now you don't have to."

"Of course I do. Or you can, if you prefer."

"Why?"

"Loose ends, Donovan."

"She won't tell."

"They always tell."

"She didn't tell anyone she was working for Carmine Porrello."

"So?"

I think about it a minute. "I'll make you a deal."

"I'm listening."

"When the cops get here, to ask you about Eva, you're going to need an alibi."

"You're my alibi."

"I probably shouldn't be seen with you. In case they have pictures from the airport."

"Good point."

"Gwen can be your alibi."

Callie laughs. "You don't think that'll look suspicious?"

"No. Because you and Gwen are going to tell them you were switching partners tonight."

"Why haven't we called the police yet?"

"You fell asleep in each other's arms."

"She's pretty hot."

"Atta girl."

"You think she'll go for it?"

"I know she will."

"You think she can pull it off?"

"She's the best grifter I've ever seen. You should've seen her with Lucky's investors. You wouldn't believe it."

"I'm willing to climb into bed with her till the cops come."

"You can't have sex with her."

"What if she's willing?"

"Then we should all have sex together."

"You can't be here, remember?"

"Maybe the cops won't come," I say.

"Let's get her in the elevator," Callie says. "Wake her up, coach her on what to say, get her naked…"

"You're worse than me!"

"What can I say? You taught me everything I know."

51.

WE'RE IN CALLIE'S condo.

Gwen's awake.

We hug and kiss, and she tells me she loves me.

I say, "What does that mean to you, exactly?"

She says, "It means I'll do anything for you."

"Anything?"

"Just name it."

"Would you cut your tits off?" I say.

"What?"

"I probably could have put that a little more delicately," I say. "Tell you what. We'll discuss it later."

We don't have much time. Callie and I explain what we need her to do. We rehearse it a couple of times. I'm right: Gwen's a natural.

I ask if she'll be okay with Callie while I'm gone, and explain I'll be back as soon as the police leave.

Callie makes her very nervous, but Gwen's been around dangerous people all her life. I'm not worried about Gwen and Callie spending time together until I start to walk out the front door. That's when I hear Gwen say, "You killed both bodyguards. Then you killed Lucky and Maddie without batting an eye!"

Callie says, "So?"

"Could you kill Carmine Porrello?"

I hesitate by the door long enough to hear Callie say, "Of course."

And hear Gwen say, "Oh, oh, oh, my God!"

I hesitate a moment. They're in the next room. I really shouldn't be eavesdropping.

Gwen says, "Could you kill Donovan Creed?"

Callie says, "For the sake of argument, let's say I can."

"Oh, oh, oh, oh, OH, OH, OH, MY GOD! OH…OH MY…GOD!!!"

"I want that device tomorrow!" I yell.

"Get lost!" Callie yells.

I sigh.

ACKNOWLEDGMENTS

When I write the Creed books, I try to put something in every chapter that I think will make my brother, Ricky Locke, smile. He's the one who tells me, before the first sale, how well each book is going to do. So far, he's batting 1,000! A hearty thank you to bestselling author Winslow Eliot, who edits my books without trying to turn me into a "real" author; and to my amazing publisher and cover designer, the incredibly talented Claudia Jackson, her wonderful husband (and my good friend) author Steve Jackson, and their wonderful company, Telemachus Press; and their tremendous staff, including of course, the hard-working, "no problem, can-do!" Terri Himes.

This one is for my wife, Annie, whose looks and personality surpass even the Creed ladies. The line in *Vegas Moon* regarding Callie being able to charge men to watch her put on her lipstick is a direct quote from two businessmen at a party, talking about my wife.

Who can you turn to when you've
betrayed everyone you love?

DONOVAN
CREED

THE LOVE
YOU CRAVE

1.75 MILLION COPIES AND COUNTING...

JOHN LOCKE

PROLOGUE

WHEN CALLIE CARPENTER'S cell phone vibrated on her nightstand a single time she leaped out of bed and threw on some clothes.

"What're you doing?" said Gwen, her bedmate.

"I'm on alert."

"What's that mean?"

Callie raced to the bathroom, relieved herself, brushed her teeth, grabbed her car keys.

"It means Creed might need me. If he does, he'll call back. If he does, he's in trouble. If he is, I could be in trouble."

"I'm coming with you."

"Not on your life."

"You can't stop me!"

"Get real," Callie said.

"What about me?" Gwen said, pouting.

"What about you?"

"I want to feel useful."

Callie sighed. "Go to the guest bedroom. Set out a scarf, a vibrator, and five random items. Doesn't matter what they are, as long as they fit on the counter."

"Why?"

"I'll tell you later."

"Where are you going?"

1

"To the car. I need to be on the street, engine running, ready to roll."

"Sounds like that man has you wrapped around his little finger."

"Don't start with me."

1.

Donovan Creed

HERE'S SOMETHING YOU don't see every day.

I'm jogging south on Las Vegas Boulevard, four miles south of the Strip, when a lady walks right smack into a lamp post.

She's on Trace Street, forty yards to my right. I stop in the middle of the intersection to look and see if she's okay. It's 5:00 a.m., and from my angle and distance I could be wrong about what I thought I saw. She backs up a few steps and falls to a seated position on the sidewalk.

I wonder if she's drunk.

I scan the area to see if anyone else is watching this unfold, but see no one. We're in an industrial area, no bars nearby, and no businesses are open on Trace. I want to finish my run, but can't leave her sitting there if she's hurt. On the other hand, I don't want to get shot. It was just last week a Vegas woman staggered out of a bar in the wee hours of the morning when some local thug took her for an easy mark and got killed for his miscalculation.

She's sitting with her back to me, so all I get is the shadow view. Her handbag is lying beside her. If it contains a gun, it won't take her long to reach it.

Thirty yards beyond the seated lady, a van slowly comes into view at the next intersection and pulls to a stop. So it's me at this intersection, the van at the next, and a lady sitting between us, on the sidewalk. The van is white, with the passenger side facing the lady, but it's dark and too far away for me to make out any details.

I don't know how many people are in the van, but I'm guessing just the driver. I mean, a passenger would roll the window down and ask if she needs help, right?

The van driver seems to be doing what I'm doing, staring at the woman. But he's got a better view, the illuminated front side of her. We're probably both waiting to see if she's going to stand, and we're probably both leery about getting shot. In my case, I'm unarmed.

Well, that's not completely true. I have my cell phone in my hand. In an emergency, I can press a button, fling it, and two seconds later it blows up.

But I don't press that button. Instead, I press a number that rings Callie's phone a single time. She's now on alert.

I start walking toward the lady.

"Miss!" I yell, loud enough for her to hear. "Are you okay?"

I wonder why people always ask that. Of course she's not okay. She just walked into a friggin' lamp post! But that's what people always ask. A little kid falls into a well and gets stuck twenty feet below the surface. "Are you okay?" people shout.

She's not okay.

Before I cover ten yards, her head explodes.

I stop in my tracks and instinctively drop to the ground to make myself a smaller target. I'm so stunned I hardly notice the van slowly backing out of view. But the fact it's backing up instead of racing forward tells me whoever's in the van had something to do with the lady's head exploding. And the way the street light hits the front of the van as it's backing up shows me something I hadn't seen before: a magnetic sign on the side, above the front wheel well. I can't make out the wording from this distance, but it's an orange logo of some sort, with black lettering. It's a temporary sign, designed to cover the actual logo beneath it. I've seen few vans with small logos painted on the front passenger side. Ropic Industries has one. And their vans are white, also.

I look around to see if anyone's behind me. I want to check on the lady, but the little voice in my head says, *Why? To ask if she's okay?*

Then it adds, *You're alone, miles from your safe place. What if the van circles behind you?*

I look at the office and industrial buildings around me, and decide to go vertical.

Running down the alley between two buildings, I spot a staircase, and take it up to the second-floor landing. There's a flat roof ten feet above me. I stand on the railing and carefully raise my arms over my head, grab the roof ledge and pull myself up to about chest height. I swing my right leg up and hook my foot over the ledge and work my way onto the roof. From there, I get a running start and jump to the next roof, then the next, and soon I'm on the rooftop of a building, looking down at the intersection where the white van had been moments earlier.

I lay flat on the roof and wait to see if anyone comes to check on the body.

While I'm doing that, the building beneath me explodes.

2.

AS I JUMP to my feet to survey the damage below, I quickly conclude the building beneath me is collateral damage. Based on my knowledge of where the woman had been sitting moments earlier, and seeing only the remnants of her ass there now, it's clear she'd been wired with explosives.

Which makes her a homeland terrorist.

I press the button that speed-dials Callie.

"Where are you?" she says.

"Corner of Landmark and Trace. Heading north on Landmark, right side of the street. Make it fast!"

"Give me two minutes."

I hang up, check the street below me, and notice several structures have been decimated.

But why?

I mean, why here? Why now? Nothing in the immediate area remotely resembles a terrorist target.

I'd love to investigate the scene, try to work it out, but within minutes the cops will be swarming the area, and I need to be long gone by then. Whatever role the driver of the white van played in all this, I doubt he's planning to hang around to deal with me. I carefully work my way down the back side of the building, thankful the blast hasn't done too much damage.

A couple minutes later I'm in the passenger side of Callie's

6

black Mercedes CL65 AMG.

"Sweet car," I say.

"You're not bleeding, right?" she says.

"Not that I know of."

She turns right, makes the block, begins heading back to her place. Says, "If I knew you were this filthy, I'd have stolen a car."

"Sorry. I was lying on something nasty just now."

"You really need to upgrade your taste in women."

"I was talking about a nasty rooftop."

"Still."

I sigh. "There *was* a woman, though."

"Of course there was," Callie says. Then adds, "What happened to her?"

"You know how some people in Vegas lose their heads, and some lose their asses?"

"Yeah?"

"She lost both."

3.

I'M IN CALLIE'S penthouse condo now. The lovely Gwen has changed her hair to platinum blond, and it's working for her. She sees me and races toward me, as if she's about to give me a big hug. But as she gets close, she stops short and wrinkles her nose.

"You smell," she says.

"I know." To Callie I say, "Can I shower in your guest bedroom?"

"Of course," she says.

I enter the guest bedroom and pause to look at a group of items lined up on the dresser.

"What's all this?" I call to Callie.

"Oops," she says from the living room. Then adds, "When you called, Gwen and I were about to have a sex marathon. We set some things out we planned to use."

"Really?" I say.

She and Gwen enter the room.

The three of us look at the items on the dresser. There's a scarf, a vibrator, lipstick, a deck of cards, a condom, three bullets, and a bird cage.

Callie gives Gwen a look I can't decipher.

Gwen shrugs.

I study the items another minute, then say. "It makes sense."

Callie says, "It does?"

"Except for one item," I say.

Callie laughs. "The birdcage?"

"Nope."

She looks surprised. "No? Then what?"

"The condom."

Callie frowns at Gwen, then says, "But you understand the birdcage."

"I do."

"And the bullets?" she says.

"What about them?"

"They make sense to you?"

"Of course."

"But not the condom."

"Not the condom."

She shrugs, looks at Gwen again. Says, "He doesn't understand the condom."

Gwen says, "Go figure."

I look at the items again.

"Ah!" I say.

"Ah?"

"The condom goes on the vibrator!"

They look at each other.

"Go take your shower," Callie says.

4.

Two Weeks Earlier...

MAYBE TAYLOR CROSSES the street and enters the park without attracting attention. No surprise there, she rarely attracts attention, though she's above average cute. Her body has slimmed down this year, thanks to her strict diet and four-hour-a-day exercise regimen. Still, if she's being honest—and she usually is—a couple pounds of teenage belly fat continues to cling to her five-five frame as tenaciously as puke on a drunk's beard.

Maybe entered the world a natural blond, but age has darkened her hair to the point that now, at age twenty, it matches *mission brown* on the wood stain color chart at Harvey's Hardware, Jacksonville, Florida.

Maybe wants to be prettier, but lacks the angular face and high cheekbones common to classic beauties. Her eyes are nice, she always gets compliments on those. People seem to be drawn to blue-eyed girls, even when there's nothing else particularly special about them. Maybe's breasts would be picture perfect...if they didn't fan out in opposite directions. But they do, and it embarrasses her when boys do a double-take, like they weren't expecting her nipples to be practically under her arm pits. No one looks better in a bra than Maybe. But when the bra comes off, the breasts fly wide right and left, like a field goal kicker with the yips.

Like the rest of Maybe's physical package, things could be much worse. A flat chest, for example, would be ten times worse. Still, there's no single feature she's exceptionally proud of.

Wait...

Her ass is nice.

She wouldn't change her ass. Not that she goes out of her way to stare at it, but it *must* be pretty special, or the boys who've seen it wouldn't make such a fuss. Not that she's shown it to many boys.

She hasn't.

Anyway, it's not Maybe's ass that's caused her problems. It's the other private place. And that part has had a *huge* effect on her. How huge? It's basically turned her into a mental patient.

Maybe walks to the area of the park where giant rocks protrude from a hill, and climbs to a spot from which she can see all around her. When she's confident no one can hear her conversation, she presses a button on her phone. When the man answers, she says, "Hi Daddy, it's Maybe."

"Hi, honey," he says.

She pauses a moment, then says, "You stopped disguising your voice!"

"Do you like my real voice?"

"Yes! Thank you! But it's been a year. Why now?"

"Isn't it obvious?"

"Not so much."

"I've fallen in love with you."

Maybe pauses a minute to process this revelation. Then

11

says, "I've been bad, Daddy."

"Tell me."

"I kissed a boy."

The man on the other end of the phone pauses.

She adds, "I kissed a boy and I liked it."

Maybe smiles, knowing he understands what she's really done.

The man says, "Where is he now?"

"His place."

"Did you leave any evidence?"

"Of course not, Daddy."

"How did you meet him?"

"In the parking lot outside a sports bar."

"Any cameras?"

"No."

"How'd you get to his place?"

"I drove."

"Where'd you leave your car?"

"I drove to a shopping center two miles from his house. Then I got my bike out of the trunk, attached the front tire to it, and rode it to his place. When I got close, I called and told him to open his garage door. When he did, I rode right in. Then he closed the door. You'll be so proud of me!"

"Tell me why."

"I wore a ball cap and put my hair in a pony tail. Put an extra shirt in my bike pack. Didn't eat anything, or drink anything, and didn't even go inside the house."

"Did you let him touch you?"

"Just my boobs. He pushed me back against his car and started messing around and when he started trying to pull my pants down I reached in the back pocket, took the syringe, and stuck him."

"And you pushed the poison into him?"

"Yup. At first his head went straight up, and his chin looked like it was going to hit the ceiling! He knocked my hand off the syringe, but the poison was already in him. He couldn't reach the syringe, so I stepped out of the way and watched him dance."

"Which way did he fall?"

Maybe frowns. "You don't believe me."

"Of course I do."

She pauses, then says, "He fell forward, face first, onto his car."

"And was he dead?"

"Not yet. His legs shook awhile, and he couldn't get a full breath. Then he couldn't get a half breath. Then he couldn't get a breath at all."

The man pauses before saying, "Did you happen to take a souvenir?"

"Of course not, Daddy! What, do you think I'm stupid?"

"You're far from stupid, Baby."

"Call me Maybe."

He sighs. "I don't like the name you've chosen, and I don't like what it represents."

"Until I decide how far I'm willing to go, I'm Maybe."

"I understand that. But I don't like it."

"But you like *me*, don't you, Daddy?"

"I love you."

"Thank you, Daddy."

"I love you deeply," he says.

"I'm glad."

"And you?"

"What?" Maybe asks.

"Do you love me?"

PREVIEW

"No."

He remains quiet, obviously disappointed.

Then Maybe says, "But I *want* to."

She tries to imagine the expression on his face, but has nothing to go on but the sound of his voice. After a few moments he says, "How are things going with Dr. Scott?"

"I don't want to talk about that. It's embarrassing."

"You can tell me anything. You know that, right?"

"You already know. You're the one who's paying him to see me. You probably get updates after each visit."

"It's not the same as asking you about it."

"I don't like to talk about it."

He pauses again. "I understand. So. Are you ready for a *real* assignment?"

Maybe's face lights up. "Yes! Absolutely!"

"I want you to…kiss…a college professor. Can you do that?"

"Of course, Daddy."

PREVIEW